SAXBY SMART
Private Detective
THE PIRATE'S BLOOD
and Other Case Files

SAXBY SMART

Private Detective

THE PIRATE'S BLOOD

and Other Case Files

Simon Cheshire *pictures by* **R. W. Alley**

Roaring Brook Press New York

Text copyright © 2011 by Simon Cheshire
Illustrations copyright © 2011 by R.W. Alley
Published by Roaring Brook Press
Roaring Brook Press is a division of
Holtzbrinck Publishing Holdings Limited Partnership
175 Fifth Avenue, New York, New York 10010
mackids.com

Library of Congress Cataloging-in-Publication Data
Cheshire, Simon.
The Pirate's blood and other case files / Simon Cheshire ; illustrated by R. W.
Alley.—1st ed.
p.   cm.—(Saxby Smart, Private Detective)
Summary: Saxby Smart, schoolboy private detective, invites the reader to follow
the clues as he investigates three cases involving hidden treasure, a string of break-
ins where nothing is stolen, and a rare comic book taken from an undamaged safe.
ISBN 978-1-59643-476-9
[1. Mystery and detective stories. 2. Schools—Fiction. 3. Pirates—Fiction.
4. Stealing—Fiction. 5. School field trips—Fiction. 6. Humorous stories.]
I. Alley, R. W. (Robert W.), ill. II. Title.
PZ7.C425213Pir 2011
[Fic]—dc22
2010029240

Roaring Brook Press books are available for special promotions and premiums.
For details contact: Director of Special Markets, Holtzbrinck Publishers.

First Edition May 2011
Book design by CoolKidsGraphics Inc.
Printed in May 2011 in the United States of America by
RR Donnelley & Sons Company, Harrisonsburg, Virginia

2 4 6 8 10 9 7 5 3 1

With thanks to George,
for the Parisian idea

TABLE OF CONTENTS

Case File Seven

THE PIRATE'S BLOOD 1

Case File Eight

THE MYSTERY OF MARY ROGERS 89

Case File Nine

THE LUNCHBOX OF NOTRE DAME 155

IMPORTANT FACTS

My name is Saxby Smart, and I'm a private detective. I go to St. Egbert's School, my office is in the garden shed, and this is the third book of my case files. Unlike some detectives, I don't have a sidekick, so that part I'm leaving up to you. Pay attention, I'll ask questions.

CASE FILE SEVEN:

THE PIRATE'S BLOOD

CHAPTER ONE

It was about seven o'clock on a Tuesday evening in the summer. The sky was the clearest, deepest shade of blue I think I'd ever seen, and the air was motionless and warm. I've just had a look in my dictionary, and the perfect word to describe it is balmy.

So, not exactly the kind of weather or the time of year you'd expect to come across a tale of blood-chilling horror. And yet, that was exactly what I was about to come across.

I was standing outside my garden shed, with a jam jar of red poster paint in one hand and a brush in the other. As readers of my earlier case files will know, I'd been fighting a losing battle with the wooden sign—Saxby Smart: Private Detective—which I kept trying to nail up on the shed door. It kept falling off. I am not good at practical things like that.

It had taken me a surprisingly long time to hit on the simple idea of having a painted sign instead. I guess even brilliant schoolboy detectives like me sometimes miss the obvious, ahem, ahem. Anyway, I'd decided on red lettering against a white rectangle painted directly on the door.

I stood back to admire my handiwork. It said: Saxby Smart: Privat Detective.

"Oh rats," I muttered to myself. I painted in the missing "e." It looked a bit squashed, but it was okay.

"Hi Saxby," came a voice from behind me. I turned to see a boy from my class at school, James Russell, poking his head around the garden gate. He looked as nervous as a kid in his first spelling bee. "I need your help."

I opened the freshly painted shed door and ushered him into my office. "Sorry, just step around the lawn-mower," I said. "Watch out for the garden hose, that's it. You sit in my Thinking Chair, I'll sit on the desk. Now then, you have a tale to tell me?"

"It's a tale of blood-chilling horror," he said shakily.

"Excellent," I said. "Begin."

For a moment or two, James cast his eyes around the cluttered interior of the shed. He was known around school as a quiet, serious kid. He had a face that looked like it had been sculpted out of assorted sizes of triangle, and a shock of curly hair that tended to sway as he walked.

"Have you heard of Captain Virgil Blade?" he said.

"Nope," I said. "But I'd love to borrow his name sometime."

"He was a pirate in the seventeenth century," said James. "He commanded a ship that raided merchant vessels all along the French and Spanish coasts. Pirates never lasted long in those waters, because the local navy ships went after them, but Captain Blade outran and outgunned them for ten years. He was the most feared pirate on the seas, and he thought nothing of killing entire crews just to get at a valuable cargo. It's said he had his own grandmother beheaded, just so she couldn't give away his location."

"Nice man," I muttered.

"When he was caught in 1675," said James, "he

swore to gain vengeance from beyond the grave. As he stood on the gallows at Portsmouth dock, he vowed that his ghost would haunt anyone who ever touched his possessions. A lot of artifacts survive to this day. His coat, a hat he wore, there's even a bottle that's supposed to contain some of his blood."

"Oh yuck!" I said. "For real?"

"It was collected from Blade's dead body by his cabin boy. There were those who believed he'd come back from the dead one day. Over the centuries, there have been rumors of strange noises and eerie sights every time his possessions were moved."

"And they've been moved recently?" I said quietly. I was starting to get a cold feeling at the back of my neck.

James nodded. "My dad is curator at the local museum, up in town. A whole load of Virgil Blade's stuff arrived there a couple of weeks ago. And, I swear to you, Saxby, I think his ghost has arrived along with it!"

CHAPTER TWO

For a moment or two, I went as shuddery as Jell-O in an earthquake. Then I leaned forward, my eyes narrowing.

"Tell me more."

"Captain Blade was born just a few miles from here," said James, "which is why our little museum has managed to get all these artifacts on loan. They're normally kept at some huge maritime archive in London. This is the most important exhibition the museum's ever held. It opened a few days ago."

"And it's attracting a lot of visitors?" I said.

James wrinkled his nose. "Well, no, not really. Even my dad admits the museum isn't exactly a major tourist attraction around here."

I remembered the town museum from a school visit a couple of years before. And what I remembered most was it being rather dark, rather drafty, and rather boring.

"So where does the ghost come in?" I said.

"For a start," said James, reaching into his pocket, "there's this." He unfolded a newspaper clipping and handed it to me. Underneath a picture of a woman who'd obviously been told to look unhappy and to pose like a dummy in front of her shop window was:

GHOSTS SCARE LOCAL TRADER

Spooky noises are making life a misery for Mrs Janet Gumm, owner of Nibblies Cheese Shop in Good Street. Mrs Gumm, 49, has heard ghostly sounds for the past two weeks. 'Almost every day, while the shop is open, I hear strange scraping and clanking noises,' she comments. 'It sounds like a spectre rattling its chains and groaning.'

Mrs Gumm claims that the weird sounds are loudest behind the counter of her shop. 'When you stand next to the cellar hatch,' she says, 'if you hush everyone and strain your ears, now and again

you can just make it out. This is ruining
my trade. I demand that the council take
action or reduce my rates bill!'

"That shop backs onto the museum building," said James.

"Well, it's hardly conclusive," I said. "Old central heating pipes can make noises like that."

"I wouldn't have thought anything of it either," said James, "if it hadn't been for . . . what I saw today."

"You . . . saw something?" I said. That cold feeling at the back of my neck was coming back.

James nodded. He was genuinely scared, and his nervousness was starting to make me feel a little jittery too.

"The Captain Blade exhibition is in the museum's main room," said James. "A lot of the most important items—well, the creepiest items, anyway—are in a very large display case that stands against one wall. I take a look at it every day after school. I went over to it this afternoon, as usual. And near the bottom of the glass, over to one side, there is now a handprint. Quite large, certainly a man's."

"On the glass," I said quietly.

James nodded again. "It's very faint, but it's definitely there. And it definitely was not there yesterday. And . . . this handprint is a reddish color."

"Reddish, why?"

"I have a terrible feeling that . . . it's blood."

That cold feeling was starting to turn my neck into an icicle. "Blood?" I said.

"That bottle I told you about?" said James. "The one with Captain Blade's blood in it? That's one of the artifacts in this display case."

"Hang on a minute," I said. "Let's be logical here. Even if that handprint is made in blood, and I don't for a minute suppose it really is, then we still don't have to start talking about ghosts. Think about it. Even a quiet museum like yours is going to have a few visitors each day. Someone has

10

obviously been looking at the Captain Blade exhibition and touched the glass, leaving a print. You never know, it might even have been left there deliberately, by someone trying to create exactly the spooky effect it's had on you."

James shifted forward in the chair. "You don't understand, Saxby. That handprint is on the inside of the glass. It's been made by something inside the display case."

That cold feeling was now freezing half my spine and turning my nerves into running water.

"It's . . . what?" I whispered.

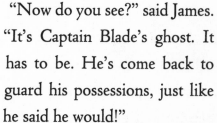

"Now do you see?" said James. "It's Captain Blade's ghost. It has to be. He's come back to guard his possessions, just like he said he would!"

I took a couple of deep breaths. "Who else knows about this handprint?"

"Nobody," said James. "Just you and me."

"Okaaaaay," I said. I wanted to sound as if I had a definite plan. But I didn't even have a vague and sketchy plan, let alone a definite one!

"I'll come over to the museum after summer school tomorrow," I said. "There's got to be more to this than we're seeing. There's simply got to be. In the meantime, I'll need my Thinking Chair. Saxby Smart is on the case!"

CHAPTER THREE

Hanover Street is a long, narrow road, and all its buildings had originally been houses. Most of them had been converted into shops or offices years ago.

The museum was the third door along, in a block of four. This block was a huge, three-story Georgian slab, with a plain-looking cream-colored stone facade looking out on to the street, and tall windows in an exact, symmetrical pattern.

To the right of the museum (looking from the pavement) was one of the street's many shop conversions, its ground floor fronted with glass. This was a branch of SwordStore, which sold plastic combat game kits at eye-wateringly high prices. (Stuff like FrogWar figures and Meka-Tek 9000 vehicles—popular with a lot of kids at school, but not something I'd ever been interested in myself; see my earlier case file *The Fangs of the Dragon*.)

To the left of the museum was one of the few addresses on Hanover Street that was still a house. However, judging by the vacant look of the place, and the For Sale sign outside, the house wasn't currently being lived in.

The museum itself looked very much like another house from the outside, except for a couple of colorful banners announcing the Captain Blade exhibition— Open Daily until September.

It was another warm, blissfully calm afternoon when James and I arrived and heaved open the museum's hefty front door. James and his dad lived in an apartment at the top of the building, while the first two floors were the museum itself.

Inside, the place was all creaky floorboards and dusty smells. Even though one or two of the interior walls had been taken out, the basic layout still reminded me of its original use as a home: there was a long central corridor, with exhibition rooms leading off to both sides, and a wide staircase leading up to the galleries on the upper floor.

Beside the entrance, in a space created by one of those wall removals, was the museum's tiny gift shop. It was overflowing with guidebooks, personalized pencils, and loads of other stuff that looked like it had been sitting around waiting to be bought for about ten years. It was also rapidly filling up with cardboard boxes. A short, round woman in a woolly skirt and a pink cardigan was carrying boxes out of a room behind the sales counter and depositing them beside a rack of cuddly toy dinosaurs.

"Hi, Mrs. Pottersby," called James.

Mrs. Pottersby blinked delightedly at us, as if she'd just heard her name read out in a door-prize drawing. "Hello there, luvvy," she said, in a voice which reminded me of sandpaper. Her cardigan buttons were done up in the wrong buttonholes, making her look lopsided. A huge bunch of

keys jangled from the waistband of her skirt.

"Do you need a hand?" said James. "Are you clearing out your stockroom?"

"All finished, thank you, luvvy," said Mrs. Pottersby, bustling over to rearrange some display of pens. She picked out a key from the extensive collection at her side and locked the stockroom door. "Just making space. I'm expecting a big delivery of novelty erasers," she said. "You never know when there'll be a sudden rush."

I looked around at the remarkable absence of people in this museum. I could imagine many things going on here, but a sudden rush on novelty erasers wasn't one of them.

"Have we had many visitors today?" said James.

"Oooh, yes," said Mrs. Pottersby, as if James's question had reminded her to share some really good news. "Three. Not bad for a Wednesday. One of them was only six months old. Awww, lovely little fella. He came in with his mom. But he cried, so they had to go out again."

"This is my friend Saxby," said James.

"I've come to look at the Captain Blade exhibition," I said.

"Sorry, what did you say your name was?"

"Saxby," I said.

"Oooh, you poor luvvy," said Mrs. Pottersby, as if I'd said I was a starving orphan. "Do you need a guidebook—only two-fifty?"

"Umm, no, I think I'm fine, thanks," I said.

James and I made our way past a display of local prehistory and a tall case containing Bronze Age pots. The Captain Blade stuff was in a large room on the left-hand side of the museum. Around the walls were various framed maps and documents, and there was a big, beautifully detailed model of his ship, the *Wavecutter*, on a table beneath a bright spotlight.

The centerpiece of the exhibition was a wide display cabinet almost as tall as the room. It was positioned up against the wall that adjoined the empty house next door, and about fifteen feet from the window at the front of the building. (Remember that—it will become important later on!)

Up as far as waist height, this huge cabinet was made of dark paneled wood, which looked every bit as old and solid as the creaky floorboards beneath us. From that point up, it was glass on three sides, the fourth side being the wall against which it stood. The case had a chunky wooden top, and the whole thing was locked in place against the floor and the wall with heavy metal clips.

But it was the items inside the case that really caught my attention. There were lights set into the lid of the cabinet, pointing down at the exhibits. In the middle, worn by a section of dressmaker's dummy, was a faded and threadbare coat. It must have once been an emerald green, but was now patchy and discolored with age.

Next to it, held on a see-through plastic stand, was a vicious-looking cutlass. Its handle was dark and worn, but its blade shone brightly in the overhead lights. To the other side was a battered wooden chest, with its lid propped up. Inside shone a pile of roughly minted gold coins.

And placed to the front of the cabinet, as if dropped there by the unseen inhabitant of the coat standing behind, was a crumbling three-cornered hat and a squat, age-darkened bottle. Just visible through the encrusted, smeary sides of the bottle was a liquid that looked black and sticky.

"Wow," I said quietly. "That's the guy's blood, I take it?"

James nodded rapidly. "So the legend says."

I took a deep breath. "Okay. Show me this hand-print."

James skirted the cabinet at a distance, as if not wanting to even approach it. He pointed to an area on its right-hand side.

I crouched down, so that my face was level with the point at which the glass started. At first, I couldn't make out anything in the glare from the overhead lights, but then suddenly I saw it.

Low down on the glass, toward the back of the cabinet, fingers pointing into the room, was a very faint outline. I turned my own hand around in front of it to gauge its size and orientation. It had been made by the right hand of someone quite large. James had been right in judging it to be a man's hand. I touched the glass. A creeping sensation rippled right through me.

Sure enough, the outline was tinted red.

No, more pinkish than red.

"What do you think?" whispered James.

"Hard to say," I said. "But I don't think that's blood. Look closely—it's got a sort of dusty edge to it. Sort of grainy."

James edged a little nearer the cabinet, screwing up his eyes a bit. "Are you sure?"

"Well, no, I'm not sure," I shrugged, "but it's the wrong color for dried blood. When you've read as many crime stories as I have, you'll know that when blood dries it goes brown. This is a kind of reddy, pinky, sort of color."

I reached into my pocket for my phone. I needed to take a picture of this handprint, partly as simple evidence, partly because my great friend and Official Queen of Research, Isobel "Izzy" Moustique, might be able to determine what that reddish substance was.

"Ah," I said, feeling inside my empty pocket, "I've left it at home. I'll have to come back tomorrow."

As I stood up, I noticed a thin line of something pale up against the base of the tall baseboard. I kneeled down again and blew at it. It puffed aside, scattering across the dark floorboards. It was sawdust.

"Have you had any alterations done in here?" I said. "Any wood been sawed up?"

"Definitely not," said James. "There are very strict rules about even decorating in this building, because it's so old and historic." I stood up again and cast an eye over the whole display case. "I ought to get a sample of the stuff that made that print, if I can. Do you think your dad would let us open this case up?"

"I doubt it," said James. "It's hard to move, because it's so tall and heavy—even Dad struggles with it. And it's locked to the wall and floor. And it's got an alarm system."

I put on my best lost-puppy-dog expression. "Could we just ask him?"

"He's not even here, he's on the other side of town," said James. "He's been out every day since this exhibition started. He's really cross about it, because he wanted to be here to tell visitors about the exhibits."

Suddenly, a little bell sounded at the back of my mind—a little bell marked: Hmm, that's a strange coincidence.

"So, where is he, exactly?" I said.

"He's assessing a load of historic artifacts. Some rich person's offered to sell their collection to the museum at a bargain price. We can't afford to turn down any opportunity like that, because this place runs on such a tight budget. If there's a chance to acquire items of local interest, then Dad has to—"

"What rich person?" I interrupted.

"Dunno," shrugged James. "They want to remain an anomaly."

"Anonymous," "I said.

"Yes, that's it, anonymous! Dad has to deal with some fellow who's this person's solicitor."

"What, and your dad's just going along with it?" I said. "Surely he's got to know who this mysterious benefactor is?"

"Well, eventually, yes, if he accepts anything for the museum," said James. "But like I said, we can't afford to turn down offers. There was an early Victorian diary came up for auction a while ago—huge historical importance for the town, apparently—and we were outbid for it by a museum in Oxford. Dad was fuming that whoever uncovered it didn't donate it to us. Ever since then he's been determined not to miss out on any possible leads."

I went slightly red with embarrassment. Readers of my earlier case file *The Treasure of Dead Man's Lane* will realize why.

"And your dad's had to go out assessing this collection since the Captain Blade exhibition started?" •

"That's right," said James. "Talk about bad timing. And none of the stuff he's seen so far has been worth buying." He leaned closer to me and lowered his voice. "We're supposed to have a proper security guard for the Captain Blade exhibits, that was one of the conditions of us borrowing them. But there's no money for one . . . Dad was going to handle the security himself. There's only Mrs. Pottersby on duty all day at the moment and her hip keeps acting up, so she doesn't like to move around too much."

Like a sudden flash of mental lightning, a nasty possibility zipped into my head. I dashed back over to the big display case and pointed to the wooden chest inside.

"Those coins!' I said. "Are they real gold?"

"Yes, I think so," said James. "Part of their value is in the fact that they were made so long ago, but the gold itself is worth loads, too. Why?"

That nasty possibility was looking more definite by the second! An idea had struck me, an idea that involved a serious crime and the museum's anonymous new benefactor.

Have you worked it out?

"I think that anonymous person is a decoy," I gasped.

"A what?" said James.

"It's a trick, to keep your dad away from the museum, and so leave this display case unguarded."

"You mean, someone's planning to steal those gold coins?" said James.

"Exactly!" I cried. "Once they're stolen, they could be melted down and turned into something else. They'd be almost untraceable!"

"But I told you, the display case has alarms and everything."

"Yes, and nobody on guard. Someone could walk in here, break the glass, and be off down the street before anyone could stop them. Mrs. Pottersby's hardly likely to be able to tackle a bunch of smash-and-grab thieves, is she?"

"Well . . . no . . ." said James. "Not with her hip. But why go to the trouble of getting my dad out of the way? Why not just raid the place in the middle of the night?"

"Well," I said, "for a start, they'd have to break through that huge front door first. And I bet there are

25

separate alarms on the doors and windows at night, right?"

"Yes."

"So, much simpler to just come in here in broad daylight. Then, all that stands between them and the gold is one piece of glass."

James suddenly went all boggle-eyed. "That could explain the haunting! Captain Blade's ghost knows there's a robbery planned and he's waked up to terrify the life out of us all!"

I tutted. "Forget about ghosts. We need to discover the truth about that handprint—and fast. Are you sure we can't get into this display case?"

"Well, Mrs. Pottersby has a set of keys for the locks and alarm, but it's so heavy I really don't think we'll be able to shift it."

"We'll show her the handprint," I said. "Then she'll understand why we need to open this thing up."

James went to get Mrs. Pottersby. She tottered over, adjusting her lopsided cardigan. I warned her that I was about to show her something mysterious and disturbing. She bent over and peered at the area of glass I indicated.

"I haven't got me specs on," she said.

She tottered back to the gift shop. Then she tottered over again with her glasses clutched in her hand. I warned her once more that she was about to see something mysterious and disturbing. She put on her specs.

"Nothing there, luv," she muttered, turning her head this way and that to get a better look.

"It's faint, but look, there are the fingers, there, you see? Pointing that way. And there's the palm. You see it?"

"No."

"Just there. Made out in reddish, pinkish stuff. Quite large, do you see?"

"No."

Her eyes blinked behind her chunky lenses. She kept shifting her head around and moving her glasses back and

forth along her nose. "I'm sorry, luv, but me eyesight just isn't good enough these days. I've had to give up me car 'cause I can't focus."

"Could you undo the locks and disable the alarm anyway?" I said. "It's vitally important."

"I really can't, luvvy," said Mrs. Pottersby, shaking her head slowly. "I'm under instructions from James's dad, from Mr. Russell. These exhibits aren't to be touched, not by anyone."

"We don't want to touch the exhibits, Mrs. Pottersby," said James. "Just the inside of the glass. Pleeeeeease?"

Mrs. Pottersby shook her head. She'd clearly made up her mind, and I got the impression that once Mrs. Pottersby's mind was made up, it stayed made up.

I turned to James. "I'll be back tomorrow, straight after school, and I'll bring a camera. We might even be able to get a couple of actual fingerprints, if Izzy can enhance the photos enough. In the meantime, you make sure your dad stays right here in this museum, guarding this stuff."

"How do I do that?" said James.

"Tell him about my theory, of course," I said.

Mrs. Pottersby was getting ready to close the museum for the day. As I passed by the gift shop on my way out, I remembered something I'd jotted down in my notebook.

"By the way, Mrs. Pottersby," I said. "Have you heard any spooky noises recently, during the day?"

"Pardon?"

"Spooky noises. Clanks, scraping sounds, the tormented moaning of the undead?"

"No, luv. But then, me ears are worse than me eyes."

"Oh well," I muttered to myself, "no clues to be had there, then."

Stepping outside into Hanover Street again, the late afternoon was so warm and sunny that it was hard to believe I'd just been inspecting the gruesome relics of a seventeenth-century pirate. Maybe the weather's why they're getting so few visitors, I thought to myself.

I couldn't help noticing the first fiery streaks that were slinking across the sky, as the sun dipped out of sight behind the tall buildings, and the overhead blue melted into yellow and orange. And, as I noticed the sky, I also noticed something else.

There was—as usual—a police CCTV camera mounted on the wall directly opposite the museum. I tend to notice that sort of camera anyway, because I find them rather creepy, but this one had clearly been repositioned. Normally, it faced down the length of Hanover Street, but now it had been turned ninety degrees to face across the road instead.

Two deductions popped into my mind, the second following on from the first. Both had a direct bearing on the Captain Blade case!

Have you worked them out?

Deduction 1: Obviously, the camera was no longer watching the street, so what was it watching? The museum.

Deduction 2: If the police were watching the museum, it seemed highly likely that they'd also got wind of a planned raid on that gold, just as I had!

I wasn't sure what to do now. Wherever the police had got their information from, they clearly hadn't shared their suspicions with anyone at the museum. If they had, James's dad wouldn't still be staying away from the museum all day. Anyway, now that Saxby Smart was on the case—ha ha!—and James's dad would soon know what was going on, that little problem would be dealt with.

However, I was still unsure about a course of action. On the one hand, I didn't want my investigations to muck up whatever operation the police were working on. On the other hand, the thought of me getting to the bad guys before the police was almost too good to resist! My guess was that the police had learned about the crooks' plans via the criminal underworld.

I decided to return home. I needed to sit in my Thinking Chair.

CHAPTER FOUR

At school the following morning, I scooted over to James before the bell for home room rang.

"Did you tell your dad about my suspicions that there's going to be a raid on that gold?" I said.

"Yes."

"Good. And about how I think this anonymous benefactor is a decoy?"

"Yes."

"Good. So he's staying at the museum today, then?"

"No."

"What?" I spluttered.

"I don't think he believes you," said James.

"What?" I spluttered again. "He does know it's me that's said this, doesn't he?"

"Yes, I even told him about all your past cases. Well, all the past cases you told me to casually mention, anyway. He said he can't go missing any more opportunities to get stuff for the museum. He said this anomalous benefactor's people seem very nice and he doesn't believe they're trying to con him."

I suddenly remembered the CCTV camera I'd noticed and told James about my additional suspicions that the police were involved. "Give your dad a call during break. He can't possibly ignore the evidence of that camera."

Speaking of cameras, I needed to borrow one from my other great friend, George "Muddy" Whitehouse, the school's resident Official King of Gadgets. I'd decided I was going to need a far better image of that handprint than I could get with the camera in my phone.

"Oh, before I forget," I said, turning back to James just as the bell for home room sounded. "Has the museum got a cellar?"

"A cellar? No," said James.

"Sure?"

"Absolutely," said James. "We could do with the extra space, so a cellar would be very useful. But no, there definitely isn't one."

"Oh," I said, a little surprised. "Okay."

The morning's classes crawled by at the speed of snail races. I was anxious to get back to examining the handprint, because with James's dad still away from the museum, that raid could happen at any moment. I needed more clues!

At break time, I made a beeline for Muddy. He was busy finishing his math homework. His work sheet looked almost as crumpled and stained as he did. How anyone can stay so permanently grubby is one mystery I'll never solve.

"Sorry to interrupt," I said, "but I need a camera."

An excited expression suddenly lit up his face. He was about to speak, but I raised a hand to keep him quiet. "Before you say anything, Muddy, let's not mention spies this time, okay? You're always going on about spy gear. I'm a detective. This is detective work. I am not a spy. Okay? Now, then. I need a camera that can take a close-up of something quite faint. Have you got something like that?"

Muddy paused for a moment, with raised eyebrows which managed to say, "Oh, can I speak now?" in a sarcastic tone of voice. "Yes," he said at last. "I have the Whitehouse SpyMaster Double-O-Eight, with undercover espionage attachment."

I narrowed my eyes. "You've just made that up."

"No I haven't," said Muddy, with a grin. "It's got the name etched onto the case and everything. I adapted the optics from the camera you used to catch Harry Lovecraft when he tried to cheat in the essay competition."

"Hmm. Right," I said, my eyes narrower than a needle's. "I'll pick it up after school."

"Okey dokey," said Muddy. His eyebrows were bouncing up and down, managing to say "Spy gear! Spy gear!" in a delighted tone of voice.

Just before the next class, I hurried back to James.

"Did you phone your dad?" I said.

"Yes," said James.

"Good. And you told him about the CCTV camera? And how I think the police are involved?"

"Yes."

"Good. So he's coming straight back to the museum right now, then?"

"No."

"What?" I spluttered, all over again.

"He still doesn't believe you," said James. "He thinks if the police had any suspicions they'd have told him already. He thinks there's no way they'd be watching the museum and not letting him know."

"Yes, well," I grumbled, "I suppose the same thought had occurred to me too. In that case, it's even more vital that I gather proper evidence relating to that handprint."

Cut to that afternoon.

As soon as school finished, I zipped over to Muddy's house, borrowed the camera, and then zipped over to the museum. By the time I got there, I was totally out of breath.

"You are so unfit," said Izzy. I'd arranged for us to meet up outside the museum, as she was keen to get a look at the handprint for herself.

"It's a hot day," I said, defensively. "The heat drains your energy, it's a well-known fact."

"Yes," she said, "especially when you're so unfit. Come on, let's go inside."

Pausing only while I took my regular squirt of anti-hay fever nasal spray, we entered the building's cool, dim interior. James had stopped at school for soccer practice, so I was hoping that Mrs. Pottersby's memory wasn't as off as her eyesight and her hearing.

"Oooh, hello again, luv," she chirped. As the day before, she was rearranging all the cardboard boxes that littered the floor of the tiny gift shop. I nearly asked her whether it wouldn't be easier to simply move all her stock back into her empty stockroom, but thought better of it.

"This is my friend Isobel," I said. "We've come to take another look at the Captain Blade exhibition."

"Hi," waved Izzy.

"You're my fourth and fifth visitors today!" said Mrs. Pottersby proudly. "We could be in for a record at this rate!"

I showed Izzy the exhibition room. Once she'd stopped going "wow" at the old documents and clothes, and "eww" at the bottle of blood, I steered her around to the side of the huge exhibit case against the wall.

Then I gasped.

Then I ran back to the gift shop.

"Mrs. Pottersby!" I cried. "The Captain Blade exhibition case! Has it been moved today? Or opened? Or dusted? Or anything?"

"No, luv, it's not been touched," she said, peering at me as if I was asking whether a pink elephant had driven past on a motorbike. "I said to you yesterday that case is all locked up and got its alarms on."

"James's dad hasn't been in there? He could move it."

"He's been out since early this morning."

I ran back to the exhibition case. Izzy was bent over, examining the glass closely. I examined it again myself, from every angle I could think of.

But there was no denying the truth.

The handprint was gone.

"Maybe James was right after all," whispered Izzy. "Maybe the ghost of Captain Blade really has come back."

CHAPTER FIVE

"Impossible," I said. "There is a logical, rational explanation for this, and I'm going to find it."

I headed for the exit.

"So, what's the next move?" said Izzy, trotting along beside me. By now we were back out on Hanover Street, and I was looking up at the immense facade of the building that housed the museum.

"The next move," I said, "is to establish if anyone else in this block has heard the same spooky noises as the lady at the cheese shop mentioned in that newspaper article."

"I thought you said ghosts were illogical and irrational?" said Izzy.

"They are," I said, "but those spooky noises must have come from somewhere. And if they were heard in a shop that backs onto the museum, I bet they were heard somewhere else too. I'll go right around this block and ask questions. In the meantime—"

"In the meantime, I'll go and find out what I can about this whole building," said Izzy. "You never know what info might be useful."

Actually, I was going to ask her where I could buy a really big ice cream around here, as I was still feeling hot and bothered. But hers was a much better idea. "Er, yes, exactly what I was going to say," I said.

Izzy grinned at me. "Of course it was. I'll call you later."

She disappeared among the late-afternoon shoppers, and I took a good look at the building in front of me. As I'd already noted, the museum was part of a group of four addresses. From right to left along the block were SwordStore (selling those plastic combat game kits at eye-wateringly high prices, remember), the museum, that empty house, and the local branch of Boyd's Direct Bank.

Backing on to these four, on the reverse side of the block, separated only by a gloomy narrow alleyway, were an almost identical set forming part of Good

Street: behind the bank was Rogers & Rogers Bookshop, next to that was Bertie's Shoe Palace, next to that was Nibblies Cheese Shop (behind the museum), and on the corner was the Bite-U-Like Café and Coffee Bar.

I reckoned that someone in any of them might have heard (or even seen) something. I decided to start with the least promising option, the empty house next to the museum.

Its windows were bare, and nothing was visible in the shadows beyond them. A red and white For Sale sign had been nailed up at a ninety-degree angle above the front door, and quite a while ago from the chipped, slightly faded look of it. There was a freebie newspaper jutting out of the mailbox in the hefty front door. With one finger, I pushed the paper through into the entrance hall. I heard a fluttery thump as it hit what I presumed was a whole pile of other freebie newspapers.

"Nobody home," I muttered to myself.

At first, I didn't know what it was that made me spin around at that moment. Then I realized that the shuddery sensation of being watched I was suddenly experiencing must have been because of that CCTV camera on the other side of the road. There it was, as before, pointing right across the street, staring, unblinking.

But why should I suddenly feel . . .?

I quickly hunted in my pockets for the camera I'd borrowed from Muddy, the one I'd been intending to photograph the now-missing handprint with. I used it to zoom in on the CCTV.

I had been wrong! Yesterday, I had seen that CCTV camera pointing across the street, and I had come to the wrong conclusion about what the police were doing! The lens of the CCTV was aimed directly at the spot I was now standing on.

Have you spotted what it was I now realized?

The police weren't watching the museum at all. They were watching this empty house.

Aha! That explained why the police hadn't said anything to James's dad.

Oh! That also meant that the police didn't know that Captain Blade's gold was about to be stolen, after all.

And why would they be watching this house? I was suddenly very confused. Watching the museum had made sense—there was a robbery being planned. But watching an unoccupied house next door didn't appear to make the slightest sense whatsoever.

There was nobody home. What could they possibly be watching? Unless the owner of the house had bribed them to keep an eye on things . . . hmm . . . which made even less sense.

For a moment or two, I wasn't sure

what to think. Did the police interest in this house have anything to do with what was going on at the museum? If so, what? If not, had I simply stumbled across something completely unrelated to my investigations?

For the moment, there was no way I could find out anything more about what the police were up to. Well, I suppose I could have popped into the local police station and asked, but they were hardly likely to let me in on whatever they were planning, now, were they?

I decided to proceed with my original plan of action. I still needed to establish some more info on those strange noises. Starting from where I was now, on the doorstep of the empty house, I circled the block asking questions and taking notes. These were the results:

<u>Location 1</u>: Boyd's Direct Bank, Hanover Street

Observations: Went in and headed for one of the cashiers behind the huge glass screen. Angry queue of customers shouted at me. Apologized for not realizing that so many people could all be waiting to see cashiers. Waited. Got to front of queue. Asked cashier if any member of staff had heard spooky noises recently? Cashier laughed. Called manager. Manager laughed. I was getting cross now. Said I was perfectly serious. Manager said no, nobody had heard anything strange, now please leave. I asked if they had a cellar. Manager said, we have an underground strongroom, not that it's any of your business, young man—now please leave before I call the police.

Note to self: Never open an account with Boyd's Direct. Don't like their attitude.

<u>Location 2</u>: Rogers + Rogers second-hand bookshop, Good Street, back of bank

Observations: Spoke to lady behind the till. She said, no she'd not heard anything unusual. Yelled up to sister in apartment upstairs. Sister yelled down, no, she'd not heard any-thing unusual either. Asked if they have a cellar. Yes, they do, but it's never used. Owners both scared witless of spiders. Door to cellar always kept locked. Thought about pointing out that spiders might crawl under door, but then thought better not.

Note to self: Must come in here more often, lots of really good crime books!

Location 3: Bertie's Shoe Palace, Good Street

Observations: Bertie himself emerged from cellar as I entered shop! Cellar used for storing stock, currently twelve thousand pairs, widest range in town, low low prices, blah blah, Bertie droned on.

Asked about noises. Yes, actually, he had heard some weird bumps and scratching sounds. Several times, over several days. Always daytime—lives above shop, not heard anything at night. Assumed sounds were being made by the woman from the cheese shop next door.

Location 4: Nibblies Cheese Shop, Good Street

Observations: Cellar accessed through a hatch in the floor. Asked if they could confirm the newspaper report about the noises they'd heard? Yes, they could. Had the sounds continued? On and off, yes, they had.

Now, was I going to buy some cheese or was I just in here to waste their time? Made hasty exit.

Location 5: Bite-U-Like Café and Coffee Bar, corner of Good Street

Observations: Man behind counter wearing an apron saying You Don't Have to Be Mad to Work Here, but It Helps. Pretended to find apron amusing in order to start a conversation. Yes, the café has a cellar—used exclusively for growing organic mushrooms, as featured in half the items on the menu. No, they hadn't heard anything strange, except maybe the woman from the cheese shop. Pretended to be amused again. Bought an ice cream! (Yum!)

Note to self: Try the chocolate flavor next time, looks delicious.

Location 6: SwordStore, back around on Hanover Street

Observations: Shop assistant appeared to take up roughly half the space in the shop. Asked if I was into collecting FrogWar figures. I said no. Asked if I was into collecting Meka-Tek vehicles, Gigablast Warriors, and Ultra-X Gamecards. I said no. Asked if I was thinking about maybe possibly collecting FrogWar, Meka-Tek, Gigablast, or Ultra-X merchandise of any kind. I said no. He said, yeah, cool, okay, just browsing, pal, cool, that's fine. I asked if the shop had a cellar. He said you betcha, it's our Games Room, and would I like to join all the other St. Egbert's pupils who were at the free FrogWar session going on downstairs right now? I said no.

Had he heard any strange noises? Yes, he'd heard some peculiar scraping and thumping sounds recently, but hey, dude, with all the FrogWar action going on in that Games Room, it could just have been a Frog Admiral and his hordes of lethal Frog Troops on the march!

Decided to leave before he could find the copy of the SwordStore catalogue he'd promised me. Apologized for dripping ice cream on his gameboard. He said, no hassle, cool, s'okay.

By the time I got back out onto the street, it was just past five o'clock. I saw that the museum had already been closed up for the day, half an hour earlier than usual.

Before I headed for home and my Thinking Chair, I had two very important phone conversations and made one very important deduction. The first phone call was from Izzy.

Me: That was quick! Whatcha got?

Izzy: Not very much, to be honest. There's only one really interesting point. That whole block was . . . Are you eating something?

Me: Sorry, my ice cream's melting. It's Cherry Surprise!

Izzy: Fascinating.

Me: Tasty.

Izzy: That block was constructed in 1771. It's the second oldest building in town, actually.

Me: Is that the really interesting point? The date this place was built?

Izzy: No, that's what led me to the interesting point. I couldn't get anything else that's specific to that particular block, just the date, so I did a search about the way things like that were built generally. And this is the interesting point. They were normally put together to a standard design. It was a way to make long rows of houses in towns and cities during the Industrial Revolution.

Me: So, the layout of one house would be exactly the same as the layout of all the others?

Izzy: Basically, yes. I remembered you saying you'd asked James about a cellar.

Me: You mean, if the rest of the block has cellars, then so should the museum?

Izzy: Yup. It would be very unusual indeed if it didn't.

Me: That's brilliant! Thanks, Iz!

As soon as I flipped the phone shut, my mind started racing like a runaway train. Then I started flicking back through my notes.

With the exception of the empty house, I'd been able to confirm that every address in the block had a cellar (whether it was used or not!). So why did the museum not have one?

Unless . . . ?

I thought back carefully, going over each of the locations I'd visited. Now, then, where was the entrance to each cellar? I closed my eyes, my fingers wandering in midair as I walked myself back around the block in my head.

The bank . . . Don't know, didn't see. The manager simply said there was an underground strongroom. The bookshop . . . through the door, over to the far left, about fifteen feet from the front. The shoe shop . . . left, by that rack of wellies, behind that big pillar. And next door . . . the same! Far left, midway down the shop! And again at the café! And yet again in SwordStore!

In every case, the way down to the cellar was in precisely the same spot, just as Izzy's info would suggest.

It was at this point that I made the very important deduction I mentioned a couple of pages back. With my heart thumping, I worked out the exact place in the museum where the entrance to the cellar should have been. I thought back to yesterday's visit to the museum with James.

I pinpointed it instantly. Have you spotted it too?

Under that huge exhibition case in the Captain Blade room! The cheese shop had a hatch in the floor—why not the museum as well? The exhibition case was certainly big enough to cover something like that.

It was now time for the second of those very important phone conversations. I called James.

Me: Where are you?

James: I've just finished soccer practice. I'm on my way home.

Me: I've made a vital discovery. The museum does have a cellar!

James: Oh, you're not still going on about that, are you? I've told you. There! Is! No! Cellar!

Me: I worked it out. The entrance is under that big Captain Blade exhibition case.

James (laughs): No it isn't! I've seen under that case loads of times.

Me: Oh. Have you?

James: Yes. I've often helped arrange the displays in it. I've seen it moved right out across the room. The only thing underneath that case is the floor.

Me: No, there must be a hatch, or a handle, or some sort of hidden locking mechanism.

James: I'm telling you, there isn't. It's just floorboards. Big, plain floorboards. Very old ones, at that. Look, I've lived in that building my entire life. My dad's been curator of the museum for nearly fifteen years. Mrs. Pottersby's been on the staff there for well over thirty years. Don't you think, maybe, we'd know if there was a hatch?

Me: Umm . . . well . . . yes, I suppose so. But it makes no sense for the museum—

James: There is nothing there. Got it?

Me: By the way, speaking of things that aren't there, when you get back you'll find that the handprint has vanished.

James (sudden panic): It's gone? How?

Me: Er, okay, see you tomorrow!

James: It's the ghost! The ghost! It's real! Oh my—
Me: Umm, byeeeee!

I took another look at the outside of the museum, with its banners announcing the Captain Blade exhibition shifting gently in the early evening breeze. For a minute or two, I thought I ought to stick around, wait for James and his dad to return home, and see if we could get that case shifted anyway.

But I quickly changed my mind. Just when I thought my investigations were getting somewhere, everything seemed to be unraveling. The police weren't watching the museum. Apparently there wasn't a cellar. Exactly how many wrong trees was I barking up? I didn't seem to have anything definite to go on at all.

I headed for home, my brain swirling with questions, pirates, and ghosts. I'd been wrong several times that day, but little did I know that my next thought was going to turn out to be more wrong than I could have possibly imagined.

Oh well, I thought to myself, I don't suppose much is going to happen overnight.

CHAPTER SIX

By midmorning the next day, the news was all over school. Muddy and some of the others from my class were in the IT Room shortly after assembly, and they happened to read the local news Web site. The printout got passed from person to person, and arrived in my hands during break. It said:

BANK RAID BAFFLES POLICE

Hanover Street was the scene of a major police operation this morning, as it was revealed that Boyd's Direct Bank had been robbed during the night. The dramatic robbery, which took place at an as-yet-unknown time during the early hours, saw crooks break into the bank's strongroom, located below street level. A wall had been partially demolished, which connected the strongroom to the cellar of an empty property located next door to the bank.

The thieves are thought to have entered the strongroom through this hole, and escaped using the same route.

Police raided the empty house shortly before 8 a.m., but found no sign of either the thieves or the cash and valuables stolen from the strongroom. Debris from the demolished wall was found to be scattered thickly across the cellar floor. Forensic experts will spend the next three weeks examining the rubble for clues. CCTV footage of the area has already been checked and is said by reliable sources to show nobody entering or leaving the empty house. Security cameras inside the bank's Customer Services area also showed nobody entering or leaving. In a surprise development, it was revealed that the police had received advance information relating to a possible bank robbery several weeks ago, and had mounted a major surveillance operation. The crooks appear to have foiled this operation completely. A police spokesman has been forced to admit that they are also baffled by the way in which the robbery was carried out. 'Taking out a thick connecting wall like that takes hours and is very noisy and disruptive,' he said. 'This robbery appears to have been carried out in silence. No local resident was disturbed during the night. We have no clue as to how the thieves managed to achieve this, or even how they managed to get in and out of the empty property adjoining the bank.' The robbery was discovered by the bank's manager, 47-year-old Mr Adrian Shadbolt, when he arrived for work at around 7:30 a.m. 'I was terribly shocked,' he stated. 'The police had informed me of their surveillance operation, but I never believed anyone could break into our strongroom without being discovered. I am deeply upset. I am also deeply angry that the police seem to have not the slightest idea what to do now.' Mr Shadbolt is being comforted with cups of tea by his loyal staff. This daring robbery is certainly the most serious crime to hit the town in many years. Unofficial estimates put the value of the cash and other stolen items at no less than one million pounds. Given the baffling nature of the raid, awkward questions relating to the competence of the police's surveillance operation and earlier intelligence reports are certain to be asked.

As I finished reading the article, a whole crowd of questions and possibilities started jostling for attention in my mind. How did those crooks get in and out of the empty house? Last term, when builders had knocked through a wall to make extra space in the school office, they'd taken all day and used enormous, deafening brick-saw-type machines, so how could those thieves demolish a wall without anyone hearing?

What puzzled me most was connecting this robbery up with all the goings-on at the museum. There had to be a connection. This robbery was far too much of a coincidence to be unrelated to the mystery of Captain Blade's ghost.

Or was it? Was I looking for a connection that wasn't really there? Just because a serious crime had happened right on the museum's doorstep, did it follow that the ghostly sounds and the vanishing handprint were part of the same problem?

I had the distinct feeling that answers were hiding just out of sight, or at least that there were factors involved in all this that I wasn't quite fitting together correctly. However, everything became clear when I bumped into James in the lunch line.

The servers were busy slopping mashed potato onto our plates and some greenish stuff that looked like it might be broccoli, when I noticed James a couple of places ahead of me.

"Hi!" I called. "Did you read that news thing?"

"Yes," said James, "there were police cars all over the road when I left home this morning. Quite exciting, really. It's turning out to be a day full of surprises!"

"Why's that?" I said.

"Pie or stew?" barked the server. I looked at the two metal trays in front of me, full of brownish stuff. They both appeared to be identical.

"Pie, please," I said.

Splat. Brownish stuff. I caught up with James as we looked for somewhere to sit.

"So, why's today full of surprises?" I said.

"Dad thought he was going to be back pretty late tonight, from assessing that anomalous benefactor's stuff—"

"Anonymous."

"—so I was going to go over to my cousin's after school. But Dad called to say he's back at the museum already."

"Why's that?" I said.

James shrugged. "No more stuff to assess. He said there was just a note waiting for him at the office he has to go to, saying that's all, thanks very much. He's fuming. There wasn't one single item worth buying."

An alarm bell suddenly sounded. Nothing to do with lunchtime, this was in my head.

"Today of all days," I muttered to myself.

"Looks like you were wrong about that being a decoy," said James. "The gold's safe and sound. Maybe the ghost of Captain Blade will settle down now. Maybe that's why the handprint disappeared. It's just such a shame about Mrs. Pottersby."

"Mrs. Pottersby?"

"Yes, that's another of today's surprises. When Dad got back, Mrs. Pottersby handed him her resignation. She's leaving the museum at the end of the week. She's retiring."

Now I had two alarms clanging away in my head. "She's what?"

"Dad's fuming about that, too. Like I said to you yesterday, she's been there thirty-odd years. Dad says it'll cost a small fortune to hire another—"

"That's it!" I cried.

I almost dropped my tray. I bustled James over to the nearest table and told him to get his food down his neck, fast.

"Why?" he said.

"I know exactly what's been going on," I said, shoveling mashed potato into my mouth. "Call your dad back, tell him to shut the museum. Now! He mustn't let anyone in or out!"

"He won't do that!" cried James with a laugh. "You obviously weren't right about that anomalous benefactor being a decoy, so he's not going to start closing the museum on your say-so, is he?"

"Tell him if he doesn't, he might find that the police will soon be wanting to question him about that bank robbery!"

James blinked at me. "What? That's crazy."

"I'm serious!" I cried, flipping down a couple of quick mouthfuls of greenish stuff. "Oh, tell him whatever you like, but it's vital that the museum is locked up right away! Come on!"

I stood up to go.

"We must hurry to the school office," I said. "We've got to get permission to go out of school and over to the museum right this minute. There's not a second to lose!"

"But I haven't finished my pie yet," wailed James.

I almost had to drag him away. He kept his plate and fork with him all the time we were dashing to the office.

The whole Captain Blade/bank robbery situation was now crystal clear. It was a complex scheme carried out with ruthless efficiency. And the entire case hinged on three things:

1. The vanishing of the handprint.
2. The stockroom of the museum gift shop.
3. That sawdust I found on the museum floor.

How much of it have you pieced together?

CHAPTER SEVEN

Thanks solely to my reputation as a detective, the principal (reluctantly) let us out of school, and James and I got to the museum about half an hour later. We ran most of the way there. By the time we arrived I was even more exhausted and breathless than I had been the previous afternoon! Oh, come oooon, it was another very warm day!

"Wow, you really are unfit," said James.

"Shut yer face," I gasped, wheezily.

"Seriously, you should get more exercise," muttered James.

The area around the bank was cordoned off with lengths of striped blue and white tape. Two police cars were parked at the roadside, and several officers were milling about, talking into radios and sipping mugs of tea.

We hurried into the museum. As James had predicted, the museum was still very much open for business. Mrs. Pottersby was pottering about in the gift shop, as usual, cardboard boxes piled up higher than ever.

"Are there any visitors in here?" I wheezed.

"Not at the moment, luv, but I'm expecting an afternoon rush," said Mrs. Pottersby.

"Right," I said to James, "shut the front door."

"You can't do that!" cried Mrs. Pottersby suddenly. "I'm expecting a delivery of novelty pencil sharpeners at any minute!"

"Are there any other exits?" I said.

"Well, no," said James, "not unless you climb out of a window."

"What's going on?" said a deep voice, approaching from the direction of the exhibition rooms. James's dad appeared, duster in one hand and clipboard in the other. He was a large man, in a brown jacket with leather patches on the elbows. He had a mustache like a sad and hairy caterpillar, and a fleshy neck that cuddled up tightly to the collar of his smart shirt.

"Dad, this is Saxby," said James.

"Ah!" said James's dad, eyeing me as if I was a shard of ancient pottery. "So, you're Saxby Smart, are you? I wanted a word with you about all these wild accusations you seem to be throwing around."

"Listen, please!" I cried, still slightly out of breath. "Just give me a few minutes. Close the museum, stop anyone from coming in, and I'll give you a complete explanation of what's been going on, I promise. If, after that, what I say turns out to be wrong, or you don't believe me, then fine. March me back to school, complain to the principal, anything you like. Just please give me the benefit of the doubt for a few minutes."

He stared at me for a moment or two, as if I was a shard of ancient pottery that needed the mud scraped off it. Then he let out a long sigh. "Oh, very well. Shut the door, would you, please, Mrs. Pottersby?"

"If I miss my delivery, I will not be pleased," grumbled Mrs. Pottersby, unhooking her bunch of keys from her waistband.

Two minutes later, we were assembled in the Captain Blade exhibition room. Mrs. Pottersby stood close to the window, keeping an eye out for delivery vans.

"Now then," said James's dad. "What exactly is all this about?"

"It's about that bank robbery," I said.

"That bank robbery is a very serious business," said James's dad, "but it can't possibly have anything to do with this museum."

"On the contrary," I said. "If this museum wasn't here, that robbery would never have happened."

"I beg your pardon?" said James's dad quietly. "What sort of accusations are you making now?"

I felt I was skating on thin ice, sailing close to the wind, and whatever other metaphors there are for risking disaster. "I'll start," I said, "by simply saying that you don't, I'm afraid, know this building as well as you think you do. Underneath us, right here, where we're standing, there is a large cellar."

"Oh, for goodness sake, Saxby," said James. "When are you going to let that one go?"

"You're utterly mistaken," said James's dad.

"Just move that big exhibition case," I said. "And I'll prove to you I'm right."

"I told you," said James. "The only thing under that case is the floor!"

"And I'm telling you, there is an entrance to a cellar," I said. "Let's just move this case and see. If I'm wrong, then feel free to tell the whole school and I'll be the butt of everyone's jokes for the rest of the term."

James's dad sighed again. "Fine. If it'll put an end to it, then fine. Mrs. Pottersby, would you do the honors and unlock the bolts?"

"The poor luvvy sounds a bit soft in the head, if you ask me," said Mrs. Pottersby.

"Quite possibly," said James's dad. "But let's clear this up once and for all."

"Send him packing, I would," grumbled Mrs. Pottersby. She fiddled with her mass of keys. "I don't think I've got the right ones with me."

"That's them," said James, pointing to a clump of keys with red plastic tags attached to them. "Here, I'll do it if you like."

He took the hefty key ring and, one by one, unlocked the metal catches that held the enormous exhibition case in place. Then he disabled the case's alarm system with a separate key slotted into the side.

James's dad took a firm grip on the case and heaved it aside. His face rippled through various shades of pink and purple as he slid the case away from the wall. Behind the glass, the relics of Captain Virgil Blade's life of piracy—his clothes and gold, his sword, the bottle of his blood—wobbled around a bit, but stayed in their positions. After a minute or two of grunting effort, he'd swung it around almost ninety degrees, exposing the area that had been beneath it.

And there, in the floor, was a makeshift hatch. The floorboards had been cut through, and a small hole drilled to provide something to pull the hatch up by.

"What . . . the . . . ?" cried James's dad. He also cried

one or two other things, but I won't repeat them here.

He bent down and hooked two fingers into the drilled hole. He raised the hatch, and it bumped open against the nearby wall. Below the hatch was a set of stone steps leading down into absolute darkness.

"I . . . I . . . I had this case out only the other week," spluttered James's dad. "When we put all the Captain Blade exhibits in it. This wasn't here. This was not here!"

"Someone's cut into the floorboards," said James. "Saxby, how could you possibly know this was here?"

"For the simple reason that it had to be," I said. "I should have realized the moment I spotted that scattering of sawdust, over there by the floor molding. Obviously, someone had been cutting up wood in here. But I didn't understand the significance of it until the rest of the crooks' scheme fell into place."

James's dad waved his hands around in confusion. "Hang on a minute. Start at the beginning. What does this hatch have to do with the bank robbery?"

"Okay," I said. "Imagine you're a bank robber. You've hit on a brilliant idea for breaking into the strongroom at Boyd's Direct Bank, two doors down from here. Next door to the bank, there's a house that's empty. And, like all the addresses in this block, the empty house has a cellar. In this case, a cellar that is just one connecting wall away from that strongroom.

"The plan? To sneak into the house one night, blast through the connecting wall, and make a run for it with as much loot as possible before the cops arrive. A kind of underground smash and grab.

"But then, something put a monkey wrench in the works. As today's news article made clear, the police got to know—through an informant, possibly—that this robbery was being planned. They put the empty house under surveillance. They could catch the bad guys red-handed.

"So it looked like the whole deal was off. Until the crooks hit on an even better idea. They worked out a way they could rob the bank right under the noses of the police and, what's more, they could vanish into the night leaving nobody with a clue as to how they did it. Instead of getting into the bank through the empty house's cellar, they'd get into the bank through the empty house's cellar and the museum's cellar.

"What do they do? They go down into the museum's cellar, then tunnel under the wall between the museum and the empty house. Up they pop in the cellar of the empty house. From there, they can set to work on the connecting wall into the strongroom. After the robbery takes place, they come back through the tunnel with the cash, filling in the tunnel behind them as they go, so that it'll be very hard to detect that it was ever there in the first place. They've also left the empty house's cellar floor knee-deep in rubble from the demolished wall, so that the police will take even longer to discover the way they got out. Result? They can get away through the museum, making it appear as if they've simply vanished from the cellar of the empty house."

"But," said James, "how did they break down that wall without being heard? And how did they even know there was a cellar under this museum in the first place?"

"And how did they get access to this room?" cried James's dad. "And how did they manage to cut a hole in this floor without my noticing it?"

"Ah!" I said. "That's the even sneakier part of an already sneaky plan. You see, the crooks realize that having to go through the museum as well as the empty house actually lessens their chances of a clean getaway. It'll take longer to get out on to the street, for one thing. The problem is the noise—and the vibrations—that demolishing the wall will cause. Someone is going to notice immediately. They won't have long before the police turn up to find out what's happening."

"So, what do they need to do? They need to find a way to get through that connecting wall quietly. Not quickly, but quietly."

"Why not quickly?" said James.

"Because they can work away in secret," I said. "Over the space of several weeks, they can come in here, down into the cellar, through the tunnel, up into the cellar of the empty house, and work away, bit by bit, chipping that connecting wall to the bank to pieces. They can remove all but a thin section of the far side of the wall, so that from the other side, the bank's side, nothing appears to change. Then, on the night of the robbery, they just pull the last layer of brick away and they're into the strongroom."

"But that's impossible," said James's dad. "Even to cut this hatch in the floor, let alone to come and go through it for weeks, they'd have to move that display case—which is bolted and alarmed."

James suddenly went pale. "Oh, crumbs," he said quietly.

"I think James has spotted the next link in the chain," I said. "The crooks could manage to move that case easily . . . if they had an accomplice, if they had someone with a set of keys who could watch out for them as they worked on the connecting wall."

James, his dad, and I all looked slowly in the direction of Mrs. Pottersby. She was still standing by the window, but her attention had switched to the three of us. The expression on her face was a mixture of anger and defiance.

"But . . ." gasped James's dad, "surely . . . I mean . . . No, I can't believe it! Mrs. Pottersby, you can't have . . . I mean, there's no way you'd . . . "

"I told you," said Mrs. Pottersby quietly, "that boy's a bit soft in the head. He's got no proof. No proof at all."

"Actually," I said, equally quietly, "I have. The handprint."

"But that was a man's handprint," said James. "And it's gone!"

"Yes," I said. "You see, it's the very fact that it vanished that is the proof. When you first came to see me, James, only you knew about that handprint. You told me about it. And together, the next day, we showed it to Mrs. Pottersby. Only three people knew it existed. You and I didn't—in fact, couldn't—get access to it to clean it away. So who did?"

"But," said James, "Mrs. Pottersby couldn't even see it when we showed it to her, not with her eyesight."

"Oh, she said she couldn't see it," I declared, "but the moment she realized it was there, she knew how it got there, and she knew she'd have to remove it. For days and days, the crooks had been coming into this room, moving the display case once Mrs. Pottersby had unlocked it for them, and going down through that hatch to continue their work. But one day, one of the crooks, heaving the case aside, dislodges the relics and needs to rearrange them. He puts his hand against the inside of the glass, leaving a print. It was a reddish, pinkish color. Why? Brick dust. Picked up from the work being done in the cellar next door.

"Now, Mrs. Pottersby saw at once that one of the gang had left a clear fingerprint. Indisputable evidence, if the police found it. So at the first opportunity, the next day when the case was shifted aside again, she had to wipe off the handprint. It was a risk, since a couple of schoolboys had already seen the print. The thing is, she didn't reckon on one of those schoolboys being Saxby Smart."

"I still don't understand," said James's dad, pulling his fingers through his hair. "Are you saying all this happened every night, while James and I were asleep in our beds upstairs?"

"Oh, no," I said. "Nothing happened at night. Someone would have noticed. Someone living in this block would have seen suspicious comings and goings, or at least heard the sounds of digging, which would have carried farther at night. No, everything happened in broad daylight, during normal museum opening hours."

"Those spooky sounds!" cried James. "People were hearing the crooks, digging away at the connecting wall!"

"Exactly!" I said. "And since the sounds happened during the day, most of those who heard them simply put them down to their neighbors' everyday noise."

"That's crazy," said James's dad. "How could a gang of crooks, even with Mrs. Pottersby's help, come in and out of this hatch undetected? This is a public place!"

"Umm, yes," I said. "A public place that gets half a dozen visitors a day. The crooks could turn up dressed like ordinary members of the public. They could carry tools with them in their pockets, or in backpacks, or anything. And when they'd finished working on the wall, they could leave, one by one, the same way they came. They'd simply blend into the shoppers out on the street. From the outside, nobody would be any the wiser. Even if real visitors started turning up, all Mrs. Pottersby had to do was turn them away, or close the front door for a while. There was nobody here to check up on her."

Now it was James's dad's turn to go pale. "That anonymous benefactor," he said. "All that business really was a decoy, after all?"

"I'm afraid so," I said. "The trouble is, I made the mistake of thinking that it was Captain Blade's gold that the thieves were after. You see, the whole Captain Blade exhibition was perfectly timed, as far as the crooks were concerned. It was all set up a few weeks ago, and it's due to stay here until September. Which gave them weeks and weeks in which they knew the floor area under the display case would be hidden from your sight. Of course, once September arrived and the exhibits had to be returned, then you'd find the hatch. But it would no longer matter: the crooks would be long gone.

"Of course, they couldn't do anything at all if you were in the museum during the day. So, one of the gang posed as an intermediary for this mysterious benefactor and kept you busy every day valuing a load of old rubbish. And then, the moment the robbery had been done and they no longer needed to keep you away from here . . ."

"They simply left me a note," whispered James's dad. "Oh, good grief. What an utter fool I've been! And I suppose, Mrs. Pottersby, that you've always known there was a cellar underneath this floor?"

"Of course," said Mrs. Pottersby, through clenched lips. "It was boarded over about forty years ago, when this place was still a private residence. The owner never used it, and it was very damp down there. I'd all but forgotten about it, until the need arose for a way to get into that bank undetected."

"Why, Mrs. Pottersby?" said James sadly. "Why did you do it?"

She pointed to James's dad. "What, you think Mr. Meany there was going to help me save for my retirement? Thirty-six years I've been here, luv, and he keeps me on minimum wage. Skinflint. Always on about his budgets. I knew that anonymous benefactor thing would get him. He's so tight-fisted, he'd never miss the chance to get something for next-to-nothing."

"I'm not exactly well-off, you know!" cried James's dad.

"So if the crooks were digging through that wall during the day," said James, "why did they stage the actual robbery in the middle of the night?"

"For the simple reason that, while this museum isn't exactly a busy place, the bank certainly is," I said. "A gang of thieves couldn't break through the wall without being spotted by bank staff and then all their careful planning and work would have been for nothing. They'd have never got away in time."

"Hang on a minute," said James. "That news article

also said that the CCTV footage from across the road shows nobody coming or going. Even if the camera was pointed at the empty house next door, it would have also been able to see anyone entering or leaving this museum, surely? And nobody did. Nobody broke in here during the night. Dad or I would have discovered it."

"Yes, that camera certainly would have seen any disturbance at the museum's door," I said. "And that's why it was so urgent that we got here quickly. That's why I needed to get this place closed, so that nobody could enter or leave."

"What, to trap Mrs. Pottersby?" whispered James to me. "Isn't that a bit extreme?"

"No," I said. "To trap the entire gang!"

James stared at me bug-eyed. "Huh?"

"Yesterday afternoon," I said, "I noticed that the museum closed half an hour early. My guess is that the members of the gang, one by one, arrived here while I was circling the block asking questions. I think they hid inside this museum, waiting for the hour to strike the bank. And then, once the robbery was over, they went back to their hiding place."

"Oh my God!" cried James's dad. "You mean, the crooks are still in here? Hiding? Waiting for the police to go? Waiting for the coast to clear?"

"Possibly. Possibly not," I said. "You've left that front door open all morning. They might all have sneaked away by now, pretending to be ordinary museum visitors, perhaps while you were off finding that note from your anonymous benefactor. But whether they're still here themselves or not, what's definitely still here is the money."

"Rubbish," scoffed Mrs. Pottersby. "Are you saying they'd rob a bank and then leave the money behind?"

"If they trusted you enough to keep them safe while they had access to this place, they'd trust you enough to guard their loot for a while," I said. "After all, if the police had heard that a robbery was being planned, they might also have heard who it was who was planning it. The gang would need to wait a few days. They'd need to see if the police came knocking at their doors. They'd need to be sure that they weren't under suspicion before they touched any of that cash. No matter how cleverly they'd stolen it, they'd only have to be found with the money to be charged with the crime."

"There's nowhere in here to hide a load of stolen money," said James's dad. "We're very short of space. There's certainly nowhere in here to hide a gang of bank robbers!"

"Isn't there?" I said, turning to Mrs. Pottersby. "Isn't there quite a sizeable space that's recently been emptied out?"

"The gift shop's stockroom," said James. "I wondered why Mrs. Pottersby had cluttered up the shop with all those boxes."

"So did I," I said. "She has been expecting a delivery. But not of novelty pencil sharpeners."

"Well, luvs," said Mrs. Pottersby, decisively, "as the game seems to be up, and I expect you'll be calling the police in a minute, I'll just pop to the loo. You don't want to go using the toilets in police stations, you never know who's been in there."

She handed James's dad her bunch of keys and bustled off, tugging at the hem of her cardigan as she went.

"She seems to be taking it very well," said James quietly.

"Taking it well?" spluttered James's dad. "That woman's involved my beloved museum in a bank robbery! Goodness only knows what's going to happen once the police start marching through here, dusting for fingerprints!"

"In the meantime," I said, raising my voice a little for attention. "I think it'd be a good idea if we checked the gift shop's stockroom."

The three of us hurried over to the gift shop. We stepped around the piles of boxes and crept up to the locked stockroom door. I pressed an ear to it and listened.

"Can't hear anything," I whispered.

"Looks like the gang have already gone," whispered James.

"Why are we whispering?" said James's dad.

"Dunno," I shrugged. "Come on, let's open it up."

James's dad brandished Mrs. Pottersby's jingling key ring. "Stand back, boys. You never know." Then he spoke loudly, in case someone was listening inside the stockroom. "Even if they're still in there, the front door is locked. There's no escape."

The key clicked in the lock. James's dad slowly took hold of the handle. The door swung open with a creak.

There was nobody inside, but in one corner was

a pile of bulging black plastic garbage bags. We approached cautiously, and James's dad flicked back the top of the nearest bag, so we could get a look at what was inside.

It was a crammed jumble of bank notes, tens and twenties. You could actually smell a papery, peopley scent coming off them, there were so many.

"Wow," breathed James. "Look at all that money! Saxby, you were right."

"Yup," I said, not able to take my eyes off all that cash. "I certainly was."

A sudden thought occurred to me. Something to do with the question I'd asked James when we'd arrived and what James's dad had just said loudly to this empty room.

"She's getting out of the window!" I shouted. "Quick!"

I dashed out of the stockroom and along the corridor that led toward the back of the building, James racing at my heels.

"Argh, she's had two minutes!" I cried angrily. "She could be long gone! I should have realized!'

We ran full tilt into the door marked Staff Toilet. Locked.

"Dad!" yelled James. "Break this door in! Quick!"

"You can't go barging into the Staff Toilet!" protested James's dad, trotting down the corridor behind us.

"Just do it!" cried James.

With a grunt, James's dad aimed a kick at the door, and it flew back with a thud. James and I raced in.

I expected to find the window wide open and no sign of Mrs. Pottersby. What we actually found was the window wide open and Mrs. Pottersby wedged firmly into it. She'd climbed up onto the toilet tank to reach the window catch, and wriggled through as far as her waist before getting stuck. The back end of her woolen skirt waggled madly at us, and her feet flailed about uselessly.

"Get me out!" she cried furiously. "Get me out!"

James heaved on one side, I heaved on the other. A couple of minutes later, we had Mrs. Pottersby under guard, sitting on a chair in the gift shop. James's dad unlocked the front door and called over to the police officers outside the bank to put down their mugs of tea and get into the museum as fast as possible.

One week later, there was a report of the robbery in the local paper. This was headed:

POLICE SOLVE BAFFLING
BANK ROBBERY

Officers Discover Tunnel

At Town Museum

So, not exactly a complete or accurate report. My part in the whole affair wasn't even mentioned. Why? Because I'd made sure it wasn't, that's why. I adopt the same point of view as the great Sherlock Holmes: my value as an undercover detective would plummet, like a boulder dropped off a cliff, if my name and picture started appearing in public all over the place. The work is its own reward. That's what Holmes always said, and that's what I say too. Besides (insert sniggering noise here!), how would it look if the cops got beaten at their own game by a schoolboy? Ha ha!

I returned to my shed and my Thinking Chair. I propped my feet up on the desk, and I reached for my notebook.

Case closed.

CASE FILE EIGHT:

THE MYSTERY OF MARY ROGERS

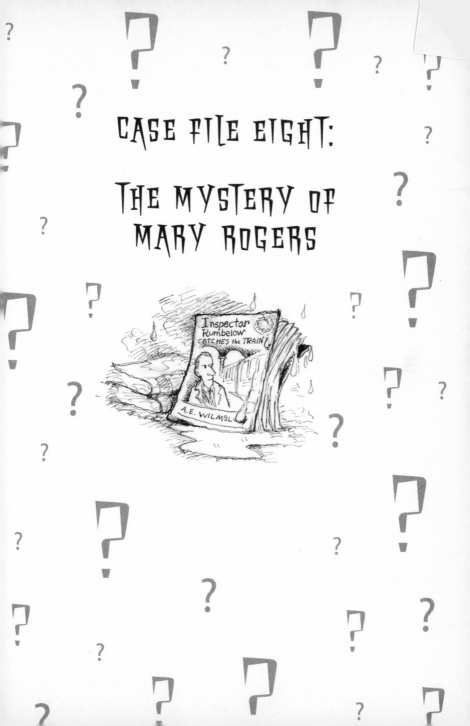

CHAPTER ONE

I stared in disbelief. Utter disbelief. I think my jaw may have hung open as well, I'm not sure.

Overnight rain had ruined my carefully painted sign, the carefully painted sign on my shed door, the sign I'd painted so carefully. The day before, it had said Saxby Smart: Private Detective. Now it said Sbleeeebsnbjllaa.

I groaned to myself. Was there anybody, anywhere, in the entire world, a bigger piece of garbage at these practical things than me?

I considered doing a bit of moaning and sulking too, but my self-pity was interrupted by a voice from behind me.

"I think you used the wrong sort of paint." A girl I knew from the school book club, Zoe Rogers, was peeking around the garden gate.

"No kidding," I grumbled. "Hello, Zoe, what can I do for you?"

"I need your help," she said. "Urgently."

"As long as it's nothing to do with paint," I said to myself, making a mental note to redo the sign later on. Little did I know that I was about to uncover one of the most heartless crimes in all my case files.

I ushered Zoe into the shed and offered her my Thinking Chair to sit on. I sat on my desk, pulled myself up into a cross-legged position, and adopted a serious-yet-mysterious expression, in keeping with the job of being a brilliant schoolboy detective.

"What's the problem?" I said, in as deeply smooth a voice as I could manage.

"My mom's in big trouble," said Zoe. Her bottom lip suddenly started bouncing around like a football in a spin dryer, and she burst into tears.

"Oh, umm . . . umm . . ." I wasn't used to dealing with that kind of thing. I dragged my slightly crumpled handkerchief from my pocket and dangled it in front of her. "Here, umm . . ."

She took it and, after a couple of window-rattling blows of her nose, she was okay again. "Sorry, I've

been holding that in," she said. I assumed she meant the tears, not the window-rattling nose-blows.

"My mom owns the secondhand bookshop in Good Street," continued Zoe.

"Oh, of course, Rogers & Rogers!" I cried. I'd been a regular visitor to that shop for several weeks, ever since I'd discovered the place while on an investigation (see my previous case file *The Pirate's Blood*). I should have realized the place was connected with Zoe—she had exactly the same hairstyle as the woman who was always behind the counter there: a sort of wild blond splat, which looked as if there'd been a minor explosion at the back of her head.

"I love that shop," I said.

"It burned down on Saturday night," said Zoe.

"Oh no!" I cried. Where was I going to find a good supply of cheap crime novels now?

"What I mean is," said Zoe, "someone tried to burn it down. They started a fire in it, but the sprinkler system put the flames out. My mom and I live above the shop, and our apartment wasn't damaged, thank goodness."

"So, you need me to find out who started the fire?" I said. "Isn't that a job for the police?"

"It's not that simple," said Zoe. "The police think Mom did it! The shop's never really made much money for us, but Mom adores the place—she wouldn't torch it. The whole shop is ruined. Every last book is either soaked or burned. Or both."

"Is the shop insured?" I said.

"Yes," sighed Zoe, "but the insurance company won't pay up because of what the police are saying. Since the shop hasn't been making a profit, the police think Mom's tried to burn it down just to get the insurance money. She could be sent to prison! And if the insurance company won't pay up, we'll be left penniless anyway!"

I sensed there were more tears coming. Quickly, I said, "Why are the police so sure she burned the shop?"

Zoe began to slide her hands up the sides of her face. "Because . . . she was seen."

"Seen?" I cried. "She was seen setting fire to her shop? By whom?"

"My cousin Joe," said Zoe. "Joe Albieri, in the year below us at school."

"Oh yes, I know him," I said. "But surely it's just his word against hers?"

"He was with six of his friends . . ."

"Ah. But could he be getting them to lie for him?"

" . . . and eight of their parents."

"Ah. Umm," I said, wrinkling up my face. "So fifteen people saw her do it. I don't want to sound insensitive or anything, but, er, and correct me if I'm wrong here, but, umm, doesn't that make her just the tiniest bit, oooh, I dunno, guilty?"

"It doesn't matter what they saw," said Zoe. "I'm telling you, it's simply not possible that my mom set fire to that shop."

"Umm," I said quietly, "I admire your loyalty, and so forth, but—"

Zoe stared up at me. "It's not possible, Saxby, because on Saturday night my mom, my Auntie Sally, and I were down in London. All evening."

"Did anyone see you there?" I said.

"Yes, about eight million people."

"Huh?"

"We were in the audience for the semifinals of Dance Insanity," said Zoe. "You know, the TV show? I've got it recorded, at home. We're on it. You can see all three of us!"

I sat silently for a moment or two. I was too amazed to take much notice of what my face was doing, but I'm pretty sure I was frowning and going boggle-eyed at the same time.

So, on Saturday night, Zoe Rogers's mother was in two places at once.

Zoe buried her face in my hanky and had another window-rattling nose-blow.

CHAPTER TWO

"Ooooooookaaaaaaaay," I said, carefully. "Now then, I think I might need a bit more info here. Tell me more about this trip to London. Dance Loony was it?"

Zoe gasped at me. "Dance Insanity! You must watch Dance Insanity! Everyone does!"

"Nnnnnnope." I shrugged.

"It's a knockout contest. Twelve celebrities partnered with twelve professional dancers, one gets voted off every week. You must have seen it."

"Nnnnnnope." I shrugged.

"It's the final at the end of this week. The only ones left in it are that really lovely girl who does the weather and the dude who plays the pub owner in Deerpark Drive."

"Dear-what?"

"The soap opera! Good grief, Saxby, you're even more out of touch than my Auntie Sally!"

"But she's a fan of Dance Barmy too, I presume, if she went with you on Saturday?"

"Oh yes," said Zoe. "All three of us are huge fans. Auntie Sally suggested going. She knows someone who knows someone who could get us the tickets. They cost her a fortune."

"And you were in London all evening, you said?"

"Yes," said Zoe. "We went on the train. The shop is only a five-minute walk from the railway station, and the TV studio is only a five-minute walk from the station in London, so it's an easy trip. We left at quarter past five in the afternoon, and we didn't get back home until nearly midnight."

"And how much of that time did you spend appearing on TV?" I said.

"Oh, only a few seconds," said Zoe, "but we're definitely there, I watched it back on Sunday. The show went out live from seven o'clock till eight, and then there was the results show, also live, from five to ten till twenty past ten. At the start of each show, the camera does this sort of slow whoosh across the audience.

And there we were, both times. Well, me and Mom are a bit blink-and-you'll-miss-us and in the distance, but you can see Sally clear as anything."

"So, what happens in the time between these shows?" I said.

"Well, not much, really," said Zoe. "The TV technical people run around a lot, which is quite interesting to see. Mostly, they want you to stay put. They don't like anyone leaving their seat. They even have a sort of checkroom thing there, where you have to leave coats and bags and so forth, because that sort of thing looks like a big mess on screen, apparently."

"So the three of you stayed put all evening?" I said.

"Yes. Mom and I got to eavesdrop on one of the judges chatting to the director! He's mean with his marks, but he's sooooo nice in real life."

"Didn't Auntie Sally get to chat with him?" I said.

"No, she said she was getting loads of gossip from the makeup ladies," said Zoe. "Apparently that actor in Deerpark Drive has got a false—"

"So the three of you didn't sit together?"

"No, Auntie Sally managed to get tickets, but not

three in a row. I was in the seat behind Mom, and we were at one end of the audience, and Auntie Sally was at the other end. She couldn't actually see us, there was a huge camera platform-whatsit in the way, but we all got a lovely view of the stage."

"And when did your cousin Joe and his friends see your mom setting fire to the bookshop?" I said.

"Just after half-past eight," said Zoe.

"About fifteen or twenty minutes after the first show finished," I muttered. "Which means that if your mom returned to the bookshop during the interval, she must have traveled at about, oooh, two hundred and fifty thousand miles an hour."

"Exactly," said Zoe. "Impossible, quite apart from the fact that she was with me all the time."

"Is there any way Joe and the others could have seen some random stranger and just made a mistake? You know, seeing someone in the shop they might expect to see in there?"

"Not according to Joe," said Zoe sadly. She looked up at me. Those extra gallons of tears were definitely on their way. "And besides, there's more to tell you. It gets worse," said Zoe.

"How?" I said.

Zoe paused for a moment. "There's evidence in the shop that the fire was started by Mom's brother, my Uncle Barry."

"Evidence? What sort of evidence?"

"There's a clear footprint inside the shop. And similar prints in the muddy patch outside the shop's back door. They could only have been made by Barry. You'll know why when you see them. But he hadn't visited the shop in weeks. They must have been made on Saturday night."

"And what do the police think?" I said, shuffling forward slightly on the desk.

Zoe sighed. "They believe the witnesses more than the footprint. They say the Dance Insanity video doesn't show Mom clearly enough for a positive ID. They think she put those footprints there to frame her brother."

If I'd been alone, I'd have let out a whoop of astonishment. What a weird tangle of a mystery! However, as I wasn't by myself, a whoop of astonishment would have sounded positively cruel. So I kept my whoops to myself.

"And what does Uncle Barry say?" I said.

Zoe's lower lip started to quiver again. "This has put the three of them back to square one," she said. "You see, my Uncle Barry, my Auntie Sally, and my mom—her name's Mary, by the way—are triplets. They're very alike, but they've never really gotten along together. Some of the fights they've had are legends in our family. The worst was about ten years ago, when I was just a toddler. Great-aunt Meg told me all about that one: my gran, their mother, was pretty well-off, and when she died the three triplets were expecting to inherit a huge pile of cash. But it all vanished, it just wasn't there. Each of the three started accusing the others of taking it, and things went from bad to worse."

"What happened after that?" I said.

"Oh, there were all kinds of horrible things said," sighed Zoe. "So Great-aunt Meg says. None of the three would even talk to each other, not for years. But then they settled their differences a couple of years ago, and things have been fine since then, mostly. Until now."

"Mostly?"

"Mom and Auntie Sally had an argument about a month ago, but it blew over. Mom lends Sally boxes of books to read before she puts them out for sale in the shop. She picked up the wrong box one day and put some of Sally's own books on the shelves by mistake. Sally went nuts, but it was all over in a flash."

"But now things are bad again?"

"You're telling me!" cried Zoe. "Uncle Barry is Joe Albieri's dad, so that side of the family thinks Mom is trying to frame Barry for something he didn't do. Joe's being just plain rude to us. Mom knows she's innocent but doesn't want to believe Barry is up to something. Auntie Sally is having to take sides, because she was with us in London! And hanging over it all is the fact that Mom's in trouble up to her eyeballs!'

Her eyes overflowed again. My handkerchief was rapidly filling up with tears and snot. As she sat with her face buried in the hankie, I gave her a delicate pat on the shoulder.

"Umm, don't worry," I said. "Saxby Smart is on the case . . . okay?"

She had another window-rattling nose-blow. "Thanks. I'd better be getting home."

We stepped out of the shed. The setting sun threw the shadow of the garden fence halfway across the grass, neatly cutting the back lawn in two.

"Your Auntie Sally is a big reader, too, like us?" I said, as I walked Zoe to the gate. "I mean, if your mom lends her boxes of books?"

"Oh, yes," said Zoe. "She kind of has to be. She's a writer."

"Oh, I see. Has she written anything I might have read?"

"Probably not. She's not exactly on the bestseller lists. Not as Sally Albieri, anyway. But she does the Inspector Rumbelow mysteries, under the pen name A. E. Wilmslow."

"WWOOWW!" I cried. "I've read all of those!"

I judged that a whoop of astonishment should be fine by then. So I whooped. Twice. It was turning out to be an evening full of surprises.

CHAPTER THREE

The next day, during break time at school, I tracked Joe Albieri down on the sports field. All I had to do was follow the ka-thump of soccer balls being kicked and the yells of "Kick iiiiit!" that he seemed to need to emit every few seconds.

"Hello, Joe," I said. "Can I talk to you for a minute?"

"Whaddyawant?" he grunted, not taking his eyes off the ball that was leaping about in the middle of the spaghetti tangle of boys in front of him.

"I'm on the Rogers & Rogers arson case," I said.

He made a sort of snorting noise. "My aunt is saying my dad tried to burn her place down. That's all there is to it."

"Well, I think to be fair, she knows we haven't gotten to the bottom of this little problem yet."

"Oh yeah?" grunted Joe. He was a short, pug-faced boy, built like one of those meaty little dogs you see tied up outside corner shops growling at people. He had the same mushroom hairstyle as his cousin Zoe, and I was coming to the conclusion that the soccer had some sort of tractor beam hold on his eyes.

"There's no problem," he said. "My [swear!] aunt did it. I saw her. We all saw her. End of problem. KICK IIIIT!"

"And this was around half-past eight on Saturday night?" I said.

"Eight-thirty-four," he grunted. "I checked."

"Would you and your friends normally be passing the bookshop at that time?"

"Nah, nah," said Joe. "One-off. Last minute thing. We went bowling. Only decided about six. KICK IIIIIIIT!"

"So, what exactly happened at eight-thirty-four?" I said, taking a quick leap to one side to avoid the ball. Joe made a flying tackle for it, but missed.

"[Swear!] [Swear!] [Swear!] We're walking up the street. Opposite side to the bookshop. I happen to look over. There's my [swear!] auntie! Slinging gasoline about, from a can! I tell the others. They see her too. We watch her light a match. Woomph! Flames everywhere. Then ten seconds later: FFFSSSS! Ha ha, her evil plot to burn the building down gets foiled! Sprinkler kicks in."

"And what did you all do?" I said.

"We saw her run for the back of the shop, soon as the flames started. So we legged it across the road and around to the back entrance. But she'd gone. One of the dads called the cops. They turned up, broke the

back door in to check the fire was out. We went home. End of story."

"I see. You didn't go into the shop yourself?"

"Nah, none of us did. There're no windows at the back, just the door, but we went around the front and had a look inside. Nothing out of place or anything. Except for the right [swear!] mess in there!"

Things suddenly looked even worse for Zoe's mom. There was a detail about the events of Saturday night that I'd forgotten to ask Zoe about. But now, from what Joe had said, I could tell that the arsonist was almost certainly not some random stranger.

Have you spotted it?

Whoever tried to burn the shop down hadn't needed to actually break into the building. They'd had a set of keys: the police had to force the back door in, which meant that it had been locked, as normal. I'd forgotten to ask Zoe if there were signs of a break-in. Now I had my answer. And it pointed the finger even more firmly in Zoe's mom's direction!

"Your dad, Barry Albieri," I said to Joe. "Where was he all this time?"

"What you saying?" grunted Joe. For the first time, his eyes flicked away from the soccer ball. "You on their side?"

"I'm only trying to uncover the truth," I said.

Joe turned and stared at me. "He was at home all evening. Okay?"

"Was anyone with him? Did he get any phone calls? Did anyone drop by?"

"No, no, and no," said Joe. "The first he knew of all this was when I got home at ten to nine. And then on Sunday morning he gets quizzed by the cops over some phony shoeprint evidence! He's being framed!" His eyes flicked back to the ball for a moment. "KICK IIIIIT!"

"And you're sure," I said, "absolutely sure that it was Mary Rogers you saw in that shop?"

He turned and stared at me again. "Are you saying I don't know my own aunt? Yes, it was Mary Rogers. She was even wearing that black and white jacket of hers. The hideous one."

I knew exactly which jacket he meant. Several times, I'd seen Zoe's mom meeting her outside school after Miss Bennett's Wednesday night book club. Mary Rogers had indeed been wearing a distinctive jacket with a sort of black and white zigzag pattern running across it. And it was true: that jacket was hideous.

"Well, thanks for your help," I said to Joe sadly. Things were looking totally awful for Zoe's mom now.

"No problem," said Joe. "You go ahead and prove it's all an insurance scam by that—OOWW! [Swear!] [Swear!] [Swear!]"

With a hollow thump, the ball had suddenly bounced off Joe's head, knocking him sideways.

I was on my way back to the classroom when the bell rang. I plodded along, oblivious to the rapid movement all around me.

Had Mary Rogers really been trying to pull off an insurance scam? One which had gone wrong because she'd been accidentally spotted? I'd wondered about such scams in previous cases, notably the incident of *The Clasp of Doom* (see Volume One of my case files for details). But something didn't fit. There were still too many unanswered questions.

By chance, I happened to get my first glimpse of Joe's dad, Barry Albieri, as school was finishing for the day. He met Joe outside the school gates. I stood and watched him for a moment or two, from the cover of a conveniently tall bush.

Zoe's Uncle Barry was a slim, slightly built man, the absolute opposite of Joe. Although he, like Joe and Zoe, also had that ka-boom of blond hair.

You know how you can sometimes get an instant impression of someone? A sort of snapshot of what they're like, even though you've never met them before? I got an instant snapshot of Barry Albieri, and it wasn't a very flattering one. There seemed something . . . shifty . . . about him, something you couldn't trust.

On the way home, I called my friend Izzy, the school's resident Empress of All Knowledge. I gave her the details of the case and asked her to have a look around and see what she could come up with.

"Dance Insanity!" she squealed down the phone at me. "That's my all-time favorite show! I'm so looking forward to the final this week!"

I held my cell phone at arm's length for a second and pulled a quizzical face at it. "Am I really the only person who's never seen it?" I asked.

"Yes," she said.

CHAPTER FOUR

I'd arranged to meet up with Zoe at the bookshop a little later that afternoon. Walking along Good Street as I approached the shop, I could see that there was a large metal Dumpster placed across the shop's entrance. The door was open and shovelfuls of mangled books were being heaved into it, thudding as they hit the books that were already in there.

It was Zoe who was wielding the shovel. She waved to me and called through the open doorway. "You'll have to go around the back! I'll come and let you in!"

From my previous case file *The Pirate's Blood*, you'll know that Rogers & Rogers secondhand bookshop was on the corner of a block of eight converted Georgian houses and that running between the two tall, back-to-back rows of four was a narrow alleyway.

To each side of the alley, there was almost nothing but blank brick wall. At one or two of the eight addresses (including Rogers & Rogers), a plain back door had been added, opening out onto the alleyway. And at one or two of the others (including the bank that backed on to the bookshop), there was a metal balcony jutting out of the first floor.

It was a dark, vaguely smelly place. Drips from a leaking gutter above the bookshop left a permanently muddy patch beside the bookshop's back door, the obviously recent repairs to which showed where the—

"GRRROOOOWWOOWOWWW!"

I almost screamed with fright! A huge, snarling black dog had appeared on the balcony above. It was followed by a tiny old man wearing a gray cardigan and the droopiest mustache I'd ever seen. He tugged the dog back by its collar.

"Don't mind 'im," he called down to me. "He won't hurt yer, he's only a puppy. He always likes to come out and say hello to anyone he's not seen before."

The dog growled menacingly at me, its eyes blazing and its teeth dripping doggie spit.

"C'mon, Killer, suppertime," said the old man cheerfully.

After a brief check to make sure my heart was still beating, an idea suddenly occurred to me. There was an obvious question I could ask the old man; one that would test my earlier deduction that the arsonist was someone who had the keys to the bookshop.

Have you worked out what I was about to ask him?

I'd been reminded of a bit from a Sherlock Holmes story I'd read called "Silver Blaze." Sherlock Holmes says: "And then, of course, there was the curious incident of the dog in the night time." To which someone else (can't quite remember who!) says: "But the dog did nothing in the night time." To which Sherlock Holmes replies: "Yes, that was the curious incident."

"Excuse me," I called up to the old man. "Did Killer there, er, say hello to anyone on Saturday night?"

"Yes, there was a load of kids and their moms and dads turned up, and then the police. Went batty, didn't yer, eh, Killer?"

"GRROWOWOWOWOWOWOWOWOW!"

"But not before that?" I called. "Maybe just a few minutes before?"

"No, why?" called the old man.

"Nothing," I said. "Just a curious incident."

This backed up my earlier deduction. If the dog hadn't barked, then the arsonist was someone the dog already knew.

The back door to the bookshop opened, and Zoe appeared. I followed her inside.

The bookshop, which took up most of the ground

floor of the building, was—as Joe had put it—a right [swear!] mess. Before the fire, there had been shelf upon shelf, right across the shop, crammed to overflowing with every kind of book you could imagine. Now there was shelf upon shelf of wet, fire-charred mush. Before the fire, the shop had been filled with that cozy smell you get from books. Now the shop was filled with the stink of damp paper and the faint odor of blown-out matches.

I wanted to say something to express how upsetting such a dismal sight was. But, to be perfectly honest, I was too upset to say anything.

"I used to love this shop," I said quietly. "Why would anybody do this to it?"

"That's what we want you to find out," said Zoe, picking up her shovel and poking at a shelf just above her head. A scrap of blackened paper flopped off onto the floor, which was already ankle-deep in similar gunk. She kicked some of it aside with the toe of her wellington boot, then scooped up another shovelful, went over to the open front door, and lobbed it into the Dumpster.

"Thank goodness for the sprinkler system," said Zoe. "It was only installed last year. If we hadn't had it, our apartment would have gone up in smoke too. Maybe even half this block."

"Hmm," I muttered, looking up at the sprinkler nozzles that jutted down from the fire-scorched ceiling.

"What really scares me most," continued Zoe, "is that it was pure luck that Mom and I weren't here. I mean, if the whole building had caught fire . . . Makes me shudder."

"Hmm," I muttered again. "Maybe it wasn't luck at all. Whoever did this didn't want to destroy the building, that's for sure."

"Why do you say that?"

"Well," I said, taking a tentative step across the ground-mush, "we know that the culprit didn't break in. If this was done by someone familiar with this place, and they'd intended to start a major fire, they'd have turned the sprinkler system off first. No, I think they just wanted to ruin all these books."

"Why?" said Zoe. "To put Mom out of business?"

I hesitated. I didn't want to admit to Zoe that, so far, everything pointed directly at her mom and the idea that the fire was part of an insurance scam—everything, that is, aside from her mom's rock-solid London alibi!

"So, who has a set of keys to this shop?" I said.

"Mom, obviously, and I have a separate set," said Zoe. "Auntie Sally and Uncle Barry have keys. Both of them help out in the shop from time to time, although, I think I told you, Barry hasn't been here recently. Auntie Sally's often here. The man who owns the shop next door has a set, in case of emergencies when we're away. Hah! What a joke! Oh, and there's a spare set that we keep upstairs. When we have students from the college working here at busy times, they often borrow those. But we haven't had any extra assistants for months."

"Are all those keys accounted for?" I said.

"Yes," said Zoe. "Every last one, we've checked. Next door's set are kept in a safe."

"Could someone from outside have made copies?"

Zoe shrugged. "'I don't see who, or why. Or when. In any case, why go to the trouble? An outsider would just break in."

"Which brings us back to the uncomfortable conclusion that it's what you might call a family matter."

"Here," said Zoe, stepping through the mush and heading for the area behind the shop's sales counter. "The rain the other night washed away the footprints that were outside, as well as the sign on your shed, but we've left this one untouched."

She led me over to a wide, deep staircase that led up to the apartment above the shop, the steps covered in tightly fitted, dark blue carpet. On the bottom step, in mud that was the same grungy color as that patch beside the back door, was the clear imprint of a shoe, heel to the back of the step, toe pointing toward me.

"See there," said Zoe. "On the heel."

I peered down at the imprint. Sure enough, there were three little gaps in the dried-up mud, three letters set backwards: B-R-A.

"Bra?" I said, wrinkling up my nose.

"Barry Robert Albieri," said Zoe. "He's one of those people that puts his initials on things he owns. Books, clothes, MP3 players, everything. A couple of birthdays ago, someone bought him this sort of little metal stamp thing that indents letters into hard surfaces, and since then he's even stamped his shoes—though of course the writing's reversed on the footprint."

"Good grief," I murmured. "You'd think that's a habit he'd want to avoid, with initials like that."

"He's always done it, apparently. He used to get into trouble at school for writing BRA in library books. But at least it lets us know for sure it was him who stepped in the muddy patch out the back."

"Yeeees," I said. "Very convenient. This is the only footprint?"

"Yes. As I said, the ones outside got washed out in the rain."

"This staircase is definitely as it was when you found it, when you got back late Saturday night?" I said.

"Yes," said Zoe. "We haven't so much as dusted it, and we've stepped carefully around that print."

I only needed to take a brief look at that dried-out footprint to realize the truth. It may have been Barry Albieri's shoe that made the print, but I seriously doubted his foot had been in it at the time! I had two reasons for thinking that the print had been placed there deliberately, and that Zoe's Uncle Barry was being framed.

Can you spot them?

Reason 1: If that shoe had picked up mud from the muddy patch at the back of the shop, how come there was only one footprint to be found? Surely, he'd have left a whole trail of them?

Reason 2: That print was positioned with the toe facing me. In other words, it appeared to have been made by someone coming down the stairs. Not coming from the back door, or from the front of the shop, but coming down from the apartment above. (In any case, the where's-the-mud problem still applied—if the culprit had come in and gone upstairs first, then how could they possibly have left this one footprint on the way down, and not muddier ones on the way up?)

"Well?" said Zoe hopefully. "What do you think?"

I didn't want to say. Once again, Zoe's mom was Suspect No. 1! Luckily, at that very moment, Suspect No. 1 Mary Rogers called down the stairs to Zoe. The two of us made our way up to the upstairs apartment.

"Zoe, have you done your homework?" said Mary Rogers, emerging from the kitchen with a tea towel in her hands. "Oh, hello, are you Saxby?"

"That's me," I said with a grin.

You could tell that Mary Rogers and Barry Albieri were brother and sister: she had the same slender build and, once again, that woomph of hair.

I have to say, Zoe Rogers's apartment was the messiest place I'd ever seen. And I've seen Muddy's workshop! There were overflowing shelves, things on the floor, stuff draped across the sofa, boxes, piles of books, and a coffee table that looked like it was about to collapse under the weight of odds and ends that were stacked on top of it. The apartment wasn't dirty, or anything like that, just very, very untidy. My horror must have registered on my face.

"It's always like this," said Zoe. "My room's spotless, but Mom can't live in anything less than total chaos."

"It's not chaos, I know where everything is," said Mary Rogers.

"It's a family trait," said Zoe. "Uncle Barry's place is even worse. And Auntie Sally's is even worse than that."

"Ah, well, Sally does live in chaos," said Mary Rogers. "No wonder I picked up the wrong box of books the other week."

"Is that the box that caused an argument?' I asked. (I was referring to the box Zoe had mentioned in my shed.)

"Shh," whispered Zoe. "That's still a sore subject. By the time it was realized what had happened, the books were scattered all over the shop. Sally went ballistic."

"She didn't try to get them back?" I whispered.

"No, I don't think they were valuable or anything, just ones she'd wanted to keep," whispered Zoe. "But goodness knows why, she couldn't even remember what the titles of those books were. It would have taken weeks to find them again, in among the thousands. All a bit pointless now, of course. They're lost forever."

What Zoe had just said suddenly set me thinking. However, before my thoughts could turn into definite ideas, they were interrupted by a high-pitched voice calling up the stairs.

"Hellooooo? Anyone home?"

"We're in here!" called Mary Rogers.

A moment later, Zoe's Auntie Sally (ooooh, the same Sally Albieri whose Inspector Rumbelow books I'd read, ooooh!) appeared, holding a large cardboard box filled with paperbacks.

Sally was, just like Mary and Barry, easily identifiable as one of the Albieri triplets: yup, same build, same hair. However, she wore a fluttery style of clothing that was entirely her own, all frilly bits and swooping lengths of brightly colored material.

"I've brought you these," she said to Mary. "There are only a few dozen, I'm afraid, but I guess you'll need to start restocking the shop somehow."

"Thanks, Sal." Mary hugged her sister, and Zoe's bottom lip started to go wobbly again.

"Hi!" I piped up. "I'm a great fan of your books."

"Really?" said Sally, aiming a smile at me that was so utterly lovely I think my insides actually went pop.

"Yes, hello, I'm Saxby Smart, I've read all your Inspector Rumbelow books, I thought they were really good, I've just finished *Inspector Rumbelow Catches the Train*, and it's honestly the . . ."

Blah blah blah, I think I may have gone a bit gushy at that point. I do apologize.

For some reason, I can't quite remember the details of the hour or so that followed. This may be because it all passed in a whirl of conversation with Sally Albieri about our favorite crime novels, but I have a feeling it also had something to do with those devastatingly brown eyes of hers. Ahem, ahem.

Anyway . . .

I suddenly realized I was running late. I'd promised Izzy I'd be at her place before six-thirty.

Before I left, Zoe asked me if I was confident that I'd soon discover the truth about what had happened on Saturday night. At that moment, I couldn't help noticing her mom's jacket, the distinctive black and white one, hanging on a peg at the top of the stairs which led back down to the shop.

"Er, yes," I said, lying. "Pretty confident."

CHAPTER FIVE

"Okay, Izzy," I said, sinking rapidly into one of the pink beanbags that were dotted around her room. "What y'got for me?"

Izzy spun around on the groovily shaped swivel chair beside her desk, scooping up a handful of printouts as she turned to face me. Specks of light from the glitter ball attached to her ceiling flicked across the floor.

"How's the investigation going?" she said.

"Not too well," I said. "Absolutely everything points to Mary Rogers trying to pull off an insurance scam and framing her brother, Barry, into the bargain. And yet she's got a perfect alibi. I've never come across anything quite like it."

"I've found some interesting stuff about Mary Rogers's brother and sister, the other two thirds of the trip- lets," said Izzy. "Barry Albieri has been in trouble with the police."

"Really?" I said, tapping my chin in the style of a detective. "I thought he had a sketchy vibe about him. What's he done?"

Izzy handed me some printouts of old newspaper reports. "He used to run a secondhand car business. A few years ago, he was fined for selling a load of stolen vans. Then, just eighteen months ago, his car lot 'accidentally' caught fire. He was trying to rip off an insurance company, and he got fined again."

I tried to sit up straight, but ended up just flopping over to one side. You just can't sit up straight on a beanbag.

"So," I said, "in the past he's done exactly what Mary appears to have done on Saturday night."

Possibilities raced through my head: Was Barry Albieri the arsonist after all? Was that muddy foot- print some sort of bluff, to mislead me? Was Joe involved?

"What about Sally?" I said. "Oh no, don't tell me she's been in trouble too?"

"Nope," said Izzy. "As far as I know, she's never had so much as a parking ticket."

I let out a long breath. "Oh, thank goodness for that. I met her earlier on, at Zoe's place. She's a fascinating woman, actually, knows almost as much about crime fiction as I do, very intelligent and well-read, it's a pleasure to talk to someone like her. I've just finished reading *Inspector Rumbelow Catches the Train*, and when I asked her about—"

"Do I detect a hint of lovesick puppy dog in your voice?" said Izzy, barely able to contain a smirk and arching an eyebrow as only Izzy can.

"What?" I cried. "Don't be ridiculous! It is possible to admire someone without going all mushy, you know." I tutted loudly. Honestly! Girls! "Come on, then, what have you found out?"

"Just that there's something about her lifestyle that doesn't add up," said Izzy.

"Her lifestyle?"

Izzy gave me another handful of printouts. "Among that lot there's an article from a magazine called Literature Analysis Today. Unbelievably boring, but also unique."

I fished out the article. There were several pages of tiny print, broken up by pictures of Sally Albieri standing around in various very large (and very cluttered!) rooms and on a long, wide driveway.

"Unique, how?" I said.

"Because she never normally gives interviews. She never signs books, she never goes on talk shows, she doesn't have a Web site."

I shrugged. "She's a very private person."

"And apparently a very rich one. Look at those pictures again."

I peered closely at them. "I see what you mean. This is her house? Good grief, is that her car? They must have cost a small fortune. No, a large fortune. No, a large fortune with an extra giant-sized stack of cash on top!"

"And yet," said Izzy, "she's only written six books in the last fourteen years, five of which are no longer available because they sold so badly, including four Inspector Rumbelow mysteries."

"Maybe she's a good saver?" I muttered.

"Most writers can barely make a living. For her to have funded all that, plus the holidays in the Caribbean that the article mentions, she'd have to be one of the biggest names in books ever! And she isn't."

"Zoe said the tickets for last Saturday night had cost a lot," I said.

"Ah! I looked that up too," said Izzy. "Judging by various Web auction sites, Zoe's auntie must have parted with over a thousand pounds for those tickets."

"You're kidding!" I gasped.

"It was the Dance Insanity semifinals, for goodness sake!" cried Izzy. "If I'd had a spare thousand, I'd have bought those tickets!"

"Speaking of Dance Loopy," I said, "it's time I got a look at Zoe and the others on last Saturday's show."

Izzy suddenly bounced to her feet. "I thought you'd never ask! Come on!" She skipped out of the room like an electrified gazelle.

We hurried downstairs, to the whopping great TV in the living room. Izzy had the entire Dance Insanity competition saved on disk!

"It was sooo exciting this week," she nattered. "There were just three points in it! The only ones left in now are that really lovely girl who does the weather and the dude who plays the pub owner in Deerpark Drive."

"Mmm," I mumbled, totally unimpressed. "I heard."

Izzy fast forwarded to the start of the main Dance Insanity show. As the theme music ended, an announcer started exclaiming, and the audience started yelling and waving their arms around. Sure enough, just as Zoe had described, the camera made a slow whoosh across the crowd.

"There they are!" said Izzy. "Ohhhh, Zoe's so lucky!"

On the screen, a shape-zipping-past that looked like it was probably Zoe was sitting in the seat behind a shape-zipping-past that looked like it was probably her mom, Mary Rogers. They were both yelling and waving their arms along with everyone else. Izzy slowed the picture down. In short, jerky movements, the camera tracked away from Zoe and over hundreds more grinning faces and arms being waved, until Zoe's aunt, Sally Albieri came clearly into view at the other end of the audience. Also yelling and waving her arms. She was in one of her flouncy, frilly outfits.

Izzy ran the picture back up to normal speed. "Those are the only shots of them you get. You can see them flash by in the background here and there, but nothing definite."

"And you see them again at the start of the results show?" I said.

Izzy skipped ahead to the live 9:55 p.m. results show. Once again, the crowd went wild as the theme music faded. And again, there were Zoe, her mom, and her aunt, exactly as before.

"Wait!" I cried. "Go back a bit!"

Izzy rewound the picture frame by frame.

"Stop there! Look! Do you see?"

"What?" said Izzy. "All I can see are people yelling and waving their arms about."

"Sally's shirt," I said quietly. "The cuffs have gone. She had those big, frilly cuffs on her shirt in the last shot, and now they're gone."

Izzy went right up to the screen, squinting at it. "Oh yes. The rest of the shirt is the same, though."

Something clanged in the back of my mind, like a gong . . .

"Can we rewind now," said Izzy, "and watch the really lovely girl who does the weather dancing her waltz? Ohhhh, she's like a fairy-tale princess. I don't know why you don't like dance, Saxby, it takes great skill and split-second timing."

Split-second timing . . .

Something else clanged in the back of my mind, only this time even louder.

Suddenly, everything fitted together.

"I think I know what happened!" I cried. I jumped up, ran for the front door, then ran back into the living room. "Izzy, can you get me a timetable for trains between here and London last Saturday?"

"Yes, I can e-mail it to you, but why—?"

"Thanks!"

I ran for the front door, then ran back into the living room again.

"Bye!"

Then I headed straight for my friend Muddy's house. I phoned him on the way.

"Meet me on the pavement outside your house in ten minutes, with a stopwatch, or something similar."

"Can't this wait until tomorrow?" he said. "I'm in the middle of dismantling my bike."

"No it can't," I cried. "Ten minutes!"

Nine minutes and forty seconds later, I was outside Muddy's. Muddy emerged from his workshop in the garage (or, as he likes to call it, his Development Laboratory), his hands splattered with oil. He handed me what looked like an alarm clock.

"That's my Mega-Timer 3000," he said. "Specially adapted. The minute hand counts seconds and the hour hand counts minutes."

"Right," I said doubtfully, scraping some of the oil off it. "I need you to walk up and down the street several times as quickly as you can. There's something I need to check."

"Why?" he said, folding his arms. He didn't like being disturbed in the middle of dismantling his bike.

"Would you believe me if I said it was the key to a mystery surrounding a burned-out bookshop and last Saturday's semifinal of Dance Insanity?"

"Dance Insanity?" cried Muddy, suddenly perking up. "Oooooh, why didn't you say so? I never miss it! Have you seen that really lovely girl who does the—?"

"Yesyesyes," I grumbled. "Not you too!"

"Do you want me to dance along the street? I can!" said Muddy.

"No. Walk. Like you're in a hurry."

A few minutes later, my worst fears were confirmed. When I finally got back home, I did two things. First, I arranged a meeting at Zoe's apartment for after school the following day. Second, I printed out the railway timetable that Izzy had emailed me. Here it is:

CHILCOTT RAIL PASSENGER SERVICES
SATURDAYS APRIL 12TH – OCTOBER 22ND

DEPART	ARRIVE LONDON
15:45	16:45
16:45	17:45
17:15	18:15
18:45	19:45
19:15	20:15
19:45	20:45
20:15	21:15
20:45	21:45
21:45	22:45
22:45	23.45
23:45	00:45

* Return services from London also depart at these times. Thank you for downloading this mini-timetable.

Enjoy your journey — and our fabulous refreshments trolley!

Pay careful attention to this timetable. The entire case rested on it. Piecing together clues from what I'd heard and seen, as well as from something I'd recently read, I had uncovered a plot that was as cruel as it was devious.

How much of the jigsaw can you assemble?

CHAPTER SIX

The five faces staring back at me had one thing in common: a look that clearly said, "None of us are comfortable being here like this, so you'd better be right, or else!"

Arranged around the cluttered-to-bursting room at Zoe's apartment were Zoe, her cousin Joe, Joe's dad Barry Albieri, Barry's sister Sally Albieri, and their sister Mary Rogers. I thought I might lean casually against the bookcase, in an effort to look confident and detective like. However, there was so much stuff piled onto it I decided not to, in case I knocked the whole thing over.

"Get on with it," growled Barry Albieri. "I don't like being here when these two are still accusing me of arson."

"Yeah," growled Joe.

"We're not accusing you," protested Mary.

"I should hope not, when you did it!" cried Barry.

"That's not fair!" said Sally. "All Mary wants to do is . . . "

Barry started talking over Sally, Mary started talking over Barry, and Joe started talking over everyone. Zoe had her hands over her ears.

I whistled loudly. They all shut up.

"Right!" I said. "Have we all finished? Good! Now then, let's get at the truth, shall we?"

All five of them went back to giving me that you'd-better-be-right stare. I cleared my throat.

"What I have to tell you," I said, after a dramatic pause, "is not something you'll enjoy hearing. It certainly isn't something I'm going to enjoy saying. But it's the truth. What the consequences of the truth will be is up to you. All I can do is reveal what I've found, and what I've found has to be the cruelest piece of deception I've ever come across."

Their stares turned into nervous curiosity.

"As you well know," I said, "last Saturday night, the bookshop downstairs was destroyed. Mary Rogers

and Zoe are facing a bleak future if the police continue to believe that Mary burned the shop herself, as part of an insurance scam. But I can tell you now that Mary Rogers is innocent."

Barry Albieri shifted forward on his seat. "You watch what you're saying, lad," he mumbled darkly.

"I always do," I said. "This case, this mystery, revolves around nothing more than simple greed. And greed for nothing more than money, at that. The central problem is this: how could Mary Rogers be in two places at once? Answer: she wasn't. She was in London the entire evening. We have video evidence."

"But that video evidence also shows me and Auntie Sally being in London too!" cried Zoe. "So that means . . ."

All eyes turned to Barry. He was about to explode with rage, but I quickly continued.

"And, although we have no actual evidence, there's no reason to suppose that Barry Albieri wasn't at home all evening, exactly as he claims. Why? Consider this. Here's a timetable of events for Saturday night. I was able to piece it together thanks to some help from a couple of friends of mine, and a remark about split-second timing that one of them made."

From my pocket, I produced the railway schedule Izzy had e-mailed to me, and the timings from Muddy's up-and-down the street walking I'd jotted in my notebook.

"Here's the timetable. I leave for London by train at 5:15 p.m., or 17:15, as Chilcott Rail Passenger Services puts it. I arrive in London at 6:15 p.m. It is, so Zoe told me, a five-minute walk from the London station to the TV studios, so I arrive at the studios at around 6:20 p.m. or so.

"At 7 p.m., the semifinals of Dance Insanity begin, live on TV. I'm seen, in the crowd, yelling and waving my arms around. My presence there, at that time, is now on video. But! Five minutes later, I sneak away from the studio again, arriving back at the station just in time to catch the 7:15 p.m. train.

"I get back at 8:15 p.m. I walk to the bookshop—another five minutes or so, roughly 8:20 p.m. I let myself in by the back door. The nearby dog knows me and doesn't sound an alarm. On my way to the shop,

I've collected a can of gasoline, and I start sloshing it around.

"At 8:34 p.m. exactly, I'm spotted by Joe Albieri and his friends, who happen to be walking past, completely unexpectedly. I light the gasoline and run. By the time Joe has reached the back door, I'm gone and the shop is a disaster area.

"I return to the station. I catch the 8:45 p.m. train, arriving back in London at 9:45 p.m. I have to hurry, but I can just make it back into the studio in time for the start of the 9:55 p.m. results show. Once again, there I am, on camera.

"At the end of the evening, I catch the 10:45 p.m. train, and get back here at something close to midnight. Oh dear, I exclaim in horror, the bookshop has been set afire. Can't have been me, I was in London. In fact, I was on camera in London. Perfect alibi."

"Zoe!" gasped Sally Albieri. "Oh my God, Zoe! How could you!"

"Itwasn'tmeitwasn'tmeitwasn'tme!" cried Zoe, in a panic.

"Oh Zoe, no!" cried Mary Rogers. "But wait! Zoe

was sitting right behind me. She can't have sneaked out!"

"And she didn't," I said. "It's possible that you, Zoe, and your mom were working together on this, backing up each other's stories. But the London trip was Auntie Sally's idea."

"Are you suggesting . . . ?" stammered Sally. "How dare you! If that idea wasn't such nonsense, I'd . . . I'd . . . "

"But," said Zoe, "Auntie Sally couldn't have planned to sneak away unless . . ."

"Unless she'd lied about those tickets," I said. "She told you they were the only ones she could get, but in fact she made sure that she was sitting at one end of the audience, out of sight of you two at the other end of the audience, so that she could sneak away without being seen by either of you."

"But why take us along at all?" said Zoe. "We might have noticed she'd gone."

"True. That was a risk." I said. "But if she was going to carry out her plan, she needed to make sure you were well away from home. And that you wouldn't be coming back until late, and that you'd be able to back up her alibi, just in case the cameras went in unexpected directions and didn't get a good look at her."

"No, no, no, no, no," piped up Joe. "It was Mary. I saw Mary in the bookshop!"

"No," I said, "you saw Sally. Wearing her sister's black and white jacket."

"What?" cried Joe. "What for? What's the point of that?"

"Sally writes crime novels," I said. "She's used to thinking these things through from all angles. She realized that, if the burning of the shop was investigated by the police, they'd want to find out who was in the area at the time. Sally knew that there could be a dozen or more security cameras on her route to the bookshop. At the railway stations, for instance, or on the streets. You told me, Zoe, how you'd had to leave your bags and coats in the TV studio's checkroom. When she sneaked out, Sally simply reclaimed Mary's jacket as her own, then gave it back at the checkroom on her return."

"I can't believe it," gasped Mary Rogers. "She was trying to frame me? My own sister?"

"I think it was more a case of covering her own tracks," I said. "She wanted to make sure that, if the police got involved, they'd look at the fuzzy pictures you get off most security cameras and make exactly the same mistake as Joe did."

"So . . . Sally planted that footprint too?" said Barry.

"As another way to point suspicion away from her," said Zoe.

"Exactly," I said. "It was a just-in-case thing, really. Mary, Sally, and Barry all live in messy homes, like this one, so it would have been easy for her to walk off with one of Barry's shoes last time she visited— the fact that he initials everything was brilliantly convenient for her.

"I have to admit, at one point I suspected that Barry had dressed up as Mary! After all, you three triplets have the same slight build, and all of you have that hair explosion thing going on! But, you see, Barry had no motive. He had no reason to do it."

"And neither have I!" cried Sally, getting to her feet, her features twisted with anger. "I've heard quite enough of this!"

"Siddown!" growled Barry. "You ain't heard nothing yet!"

"So why did she do it?" said Zoe.

"Like I said—greed." I shrugged. "I'm sure you triplets don't need me to remind you about that terrible row, about ten years ago? The huge falling-out you had over where all that money had disappeared to? I'm afraid Sally's had it all along. How she stole it, I have no idea, but . . ."

"That is an outrageous accusation!" shouted Sally. "You haven't the slightest shred of proof!"

"No," I said quietly. "I have to admit, I don't. But I can point out that your luxury lifestyle and your likely income are waaaay out of line with each other."

"My books are enormously successful!" cried Sally.

From my school bag, I took the calculations and sales figures that Izzy had given me. "I'm really sorry to say this, but I think that's another lie."

"I don't understand," said Zoe. "What's this got to do with the fire?"

Sally finally sat down again. Her face was battling itself over whether to show anger or horror.

"I've already pointed out that you three triplets all live in messy houses," I said. "It explains how Sally could steal one of Barry's shoes unnoticed, and it also explains how Mary managed to take the wrong box of books for her shop from Sally's place a few weeks ago. Sally went ballistic about that. Why? Because one of the books that Mary took and put out for sale in her shop had something hidden inside it.

"I don't know what that something was. It might have been a bank statement, or a savings-and-loan book, or simply a scribbled note. But it incriminated Sally. Whatever it was, it showed the world that Sally Albieri had suddenly got hold of a huge amount of money ten years ago.

"She was furious when she knew it had gone. Someone would pick that book up. Someone would open it and the secret would be out. She had to get it back. But how? In the chaos of her own clutter, she couldn't even be sure which book it was in! And how was she going to find it among the many thousands in the shop? By the time she'd have managed to sneakily check through every shelf, it would probably have been too late.

"She decided that the only thing she could do was destroy her sister's shop, and with it the whatever-it-was. Everything would be reduced to ashes, or soggy mush. Either way, she'd be safe from suspicion again.

Her brother and sister would never know she'd stolen that money. She could go on lying to them about how much money she was making from her books.

"It was a meticulously planned crime, right down to the false evidence of the jacket and the footprint. It only went wrong because of one unexpected thing."

"What was that?" said Zoe.

"It was what finally made me suspect Sally. The video of Saturday night's Dance Insanity shows her wearing one of her frilly shirts, but the cuffs have vanished by the start of the results show. My guess is that she spilled some gasoline on them. The smell would have given her away, so she had to remove them before she got back to London."

For a moment or two, there was an uneasy silence in the room.

"Sally," said Mary Rogers, "say it's not true. It can't be true."

The battle seemed to be over on Sally Albieri's face. Sadness had been the surprise winner. "It was a letter from my bank manager," she muttered at last. "I don't know why I'd even kept it. Sheer big-headedness, I suppose. Oh well, that'll teach me to live in a pigsty."

Quietly, I packed my evidence away in my school-bag and headed for the stairs. I felt it was time to leave Zoe's family to sort things out for themselves, now that they knew the truth about last Saturday night. It quite upset me, having to point the finger at someone I'd so admired, as well as having to throw the Rogers/Albieri clan into turmoil with such unpleasant news.

Soon, I was back at my garden shed. I tried to ignore the gooey mess that had once been the painted sign on my door and went inside. I flopped into my Thinking Chair, put my feet up on the desk, and added a few observations to my notebook.

I was reminded of another bit from another Sherlock Holmes story, one called "A Scandal in Bohemia." Sherlock Holmes, who was never one for girlfriends, ends up having an affectionate respect for a female swindler called Irene Adler. I suppose Sally Albieri was my Irene Adler. She committed a heartless crime, but you almost had to admire her ingenuity.

You know, there was another story that gave me the final clue in this case. A book called *Inspector Rumbe-low Catches the Train*, by A. E. Wilmslow, otherwise known as Sally Albieri. The Inspector catches the bad guy by proving he was on the 8:22 p.m. to Birmingham, when everyone else said he was at the theater. Funny, I might never have spotted the whole truth without reading that book.

Case closed.

CASE FILE NINE:

THE LUNCHBOX OF NOTRE DAME

CHAPTER ONE

Every year at St. Egbert's School, one entire year group gets packed off to North Wales for a week. Seven days of mud, rain, mountains, rivers, and porridge. It's supposed to be fun. It "builds team spirit," as our class teacher, Mrs. Penzler, puts it.

As you may have gathered, I'm not exactly the outdoors type. While the rest of my year group were crossing days off on their calendars and wishing the end of November could get here a bit quicker, I was facing the prospect of Countryside Week with absolute dread. Spending a week trudging through fields and climbing up rock faces was my idea of torture!

However, three weeks before the trip, Mrs. Penzler announced to my class that Countryside Week would have to be cancelled, owing to extensive flood damage at the place where we'd been due to stay. You can imagine the response in the classroom: twenty-nine "Ooh noooo"s and one (silent) "Yippee." I played along with the general air of dismay: "Ohhhh, yeaah, it's such a shame." "Ohhh, yes, me too—I was so looking forward to it," "Ohhh, what a shame," etc, etc.

Mrs. Penzler tapped her ruler on the nearest desk for quiet. Twenty-nine faces stared back at her with glum disappointment, and one face stared back at her with absolute delight hidden under a mask of glum disappointment. Silence descended on the classroom like heavy rain.

"However," she said, after a pause for dramatic effect.

Twenty-nine faces perked up a bit. One face started to droop. I was getting a terrible feeling that she was about to announce alternative arrangements.

"However, the principal has been able to make alternative arrangements."

There was a ripple of approval through the room. Oh no, I thought to myself, heart sinking, we're going anyway! We're going to end up on some mountainside that civilization forgot, aren't we? We're going to be sent to some miserable, mud-soaked corner of nowhere . . .

"We're going to Paris instead," said Mrs. Penzler.

I almost fell on the floor with relief. Then I almost fell on the floor with joy. The rest of the class was pretty happy about it too. (Even my archenemy, that low-down rat Harry Lovecraft, forgot about his normal weasel smirk and started looking excited.) It took Mrs. Penzler a couple of minutes to settle us all back down again.

"The travel company we'd booked through didn't have an equivalent trip available," said Mrs. Penzler, handing out information sheets for us to take home. "But they did have a last-minute cancellation for Paris. And with extra funding from the school's Friends Association added into the budget, the principal has decided that visiting Paris for the week would be an ideal way to boost your knowledge of French language and culture. These letters will explain all the details— make sure they're given to parents tonight, please. Oh, and before you ask, no, we're not going to be spending so much as a single minute in Disneyland."

"Awww," went everyone.

Result! So much for all that ghastly hill-walking! Ha haaa! A whole week in the City of Light! The Eiffel Tower, the Arc de Triomphe, and those really tasty little bread rolls with the chocolate bits inside!

Little did I know that, even on the streets of Paris, my detective skills would need to be as sharp as ever . . .

CHAPTER TWO

The only drawback of going to Paris was that I'd miss the trial of the century. Our school trip was going to start on the same day that the notorious gangster Frank "Iceman" DeSalle would go on trial for a list of crimes longer than a line in the post office.

There was likely to be huge media interest, and I'd been looking forward to following the twists and turns of the whole courtroom drama. Iceman's gang had made some hilariously stupid mistakes (they'd have been caught in five minutes if I'd been on the case). They were finally tracked down through coded messages they were sending each other on the networking Web site FaceSpace.

However, coverage of the trial was unlikely to be of interest anywhere outside the UK, and so I'd have to settle for catching up on events once we got back from France. There'd be the Internet news sites to read, of course, but I doubted I'd have the time for them. In any case, somehow that didn't seem quite the same, a bit like watching a movie with the sound off.

Oh well. Never mind.

So, Monday morning, 8:25 a.m. Thirty kids, plus assorted teachers and a couple of parent volunteers, piled into a coach in the school car park, drove to London, caught the Eurostar at St. Pancras Station train to Paris, got on to another coach, went through molasses-thick traffic to Hotel Marseilles, and lugged suitcases up three flights of stairs.

Six and a half hours, start to finish. Twenty-four packed lunches eaten before we got to London, five packed lunches thrown up in the middle of the Channel Tunnel due to travel sickness, and one feeble cry of "Oh no, I've left my suitcase at home" from a kid at the back of the coach.

And I don't think any of us stopped chattering from the moment we arrived at the parking lot to the moment we got to the hotel. Mostly, I chatted with my great friends Muddy Whitehouse and Izzy Moustique. Although Izzy also spent quite a while chatting with a girl named Danielle Plummley, who'd only enrolled in the school the week before the Paris announcement and was consequently a bit more nervous about going on the trip than the rest of us.

I had all my stuff folded neatly into the blue case I'd bought especially for the occasion. Muddy, being Muddy, had all his crammed into a battered gym bag with a broken zipper, leaving bits of shirt poking up all over the place. Izzy, being Izzy, had a suitcase on wheels that looked like a disco glitter ball, with her name done in swirly lettering along the side in glued-on bits.

There is so much I could tell you about the journey, about all the French stuff I saw from the train, about the hotel, about the first couple of days in Paris. Honestly, I'd fill up the rest of this book! But I won't do that because 1) I'd drone on and on and bore you to tears, and 2) none of it is strictly relevant to this case file.

So, zip forward to: Wednesday, 10:30 a.m. There was a sharp, chilly wind gusting across the city as the St. Egbert's School crowd arrived at the Louvre. Central Paris is a surprisingly compact place, and we'd walked to the Louvre from the hotel, teachers pointing out interesting things along the way and pupils having just one more try at persuading Mrs. Penzler to let us go to Disneyland. ("Just for one afternoon?" "No!")

The Louvre is an amazing place—it's probably the most famous art gallery in the world. It's a huge, beautifully elaborate and ornamented building, and it's got the weirdest entrance I'd ever seen: you walk into an enormous glass pyramid that stands in the middle of a wide courtyard and then down into an underground ticket hall.

We stuffed our woolly hats into our pockets and

unzipped our coats. Mrs. Penzler sent one of the volunteer parents off to stand in the ticket line, then gave us a quick rundown of the various works of art we were going to see and how lucky we were to be able to see them. Most of us weren't really listening. We were too busy oohing and ahhing at the glittering glass structure above us and the streaming busloads of tourists from all over the world who were flowing past us from one part of the gallery to another.

"That gives me an idea for a portable translation device," muttered Muddy. I tore a page out of the back of my notebook for him, and he started scribbling diagrams as Mrs. Penzler herded us into a line ready to snake our way toward the escalators.

For the next ninety minutes or so, we shuffled past all sorts of pots, statues, figurines, artifacts, tapestries, even Egyptian mummies. With the other teachers corralling us along as if we were wayward sheep, Mrs. Penzler led the way. She kept barking out sentences that began with things like: "On your left you'll see . . . " and "Here's a fine example of . . . " and "If you don't stop that I'll send you back to the hotel . . . "

Most of us kids tended to clump together in groups

of three or four (quite like wayward sheep, actually!). Muddy and I and a couple of others had great fun making up captions for some of the paintings we passed.

I noticed that Izzy was talking to Danielle Plummley, the new girl, again. Ever since we'd arrived in Paris, Izzy had been doing her best to befriend Danielle. However, as she'd muttered to me over breakfast that morning, it was something of an effort—Danielle seemed reluctant to talk about herself. In most people, you might think of that as simple modesty, but in Danielle it was a habit that Izzy thought was bordering on secretive. She changed the subject when Izzy asked her even the simplest questions about her family or where she lived. The only information she'd ever let slip was that her dad was an accountant.

Danielle was certainly a shy, quiet girl. She had short dark brown hair, and a mouth that seemed slightly too wide for her face, and a sort of floaty walk that gave me the impression that she didn't even want anyone hearing her footsteps. Oh well, I thought to myself, changing schools would probably make me clam up for a while too.

By now, we'd reached a series of long galleries in which the walls were filled with old portraits of every shape and size. Daylight flooded in through glass ceilings.

As we arrived at an opening that led off to the right, Mrs. Penzler halted us with a raised umbrella. "This next room," she said, "is always quite crowded. Stay together, stay alert, take your turns at the barrier, and don't linger too long, there'll be others waiting."

At first, I wasn't sure what she meant, but as soon as we filed through into the room on the right, I realized what she was talking about. Directly ahead of us, housed in the middle of an enormous wooden stand

and kept back about fifteen feet behind a set of wooden railings, was the Mona Lisa.

I don't know much about art. I always thought Canaletto was a type of pasta (ha ha, that's an art joke!), but even I was well aware of the mind-boggling fame of the Mona Lisa. It's a surprisingly dark painting in real life. The woman in it stares out at you, hands crossed, as if she's slightly amused—and slightly bored, at the same time—that all these people have come to look at her.

"Why's she got no eyebrows?" whispered Muddy.

"Gather in close, everyone," declared Mrs. Penzler, once we'd all had a go at squeezing up to the barrier. "The Mona Lisa, by Leonardo da Vinci, is the most well-known painting in the whole of art history. It was painted over a three or four year period beginning in 1503. Nobody really knows who the lady in the painting is, and over the years—"

Suddenly, a hand went up. It was Danielle Plummley.

"Actually," she said, "the lady's very likely to have been Lisa di Antonmaria Gheradini. She was the wife of a wealthy businessman in Florence, in Italy."

"Excellent, Danielle," said Mrs. Penzler. "You know about Da Vinci?"

"Yes," said Danielle, a broad grin suddenly lighting up her face. "The Mona Lisa reuses bits and pieces from some of Da Vinci's earlier paintings. He often did that. Her hands are just like those in a portrait he did of someone called Isabella d'Este, and a lot of the stuff you can see in the background also appears in a painting he did called Madonna of the Yarnwinder . . ."

Danielle kept us enthralled for ten minutes, getting more and more enthusiastic as she talked. Not only did I learn a lot about the Mona Lisa and various other famous paintings (the darkness I mentioned is due to layers of varnish, apparently), but I also learned a fact or two about Danielle Plummley. The fact that she was an expert on sixteenth-century art, for a start! The moment she'd finished, she gave us all an apologetic smile and seemed to shrink back down to her normal, shy self.

We gave her a huge round of applause!

"I love this subject," she said to Izzy. "Seeing the Louvre was the reason I wanted to come on the trip!"

About half an hour later, we were back out on the

streets of Paris, returning to the hotel for lunch. The Hotel Marseilles was located just a couple of streets away from the Eiffel Tower. (We'd been up to the top of the tower on day one—and absolutely freezing up there it was too! Fabulous views, though.)

We kept up a swift pace, partly because we were all pretty hungry by now, and partly because it looked like we'd be wanting to borrow Mrs. Penzler's umbrella at any moment. Izzy, Danielle, Muddy, and I were trailing along toward the back of the group.

"I know!" cried Izzy suddenly. "I'll put you on my blog, Danielle!"

"Your blog?" said Danielle.

"Yes, on my FaceSpace page," said Izzy. "I thought I'd upload a couple of reports on the trip so far. I'm going to include some of the photos."

She patted her pocket, out of which hung the carrying strap of the school's camera. On the last afternoon of classes before we'd left for France, Mrs. Penzler had given Izzy the job of being our official photographer for the week. She was to take pictures of anything and everything interesting, and we'd all use the photos for classroom project work after our return home.

"Mrs. Penzler's memory card was full of pictures of the school play," said Izzy. "So I'm using one of my own. I've already taken over a hundred shots. I'm going to upload news of everything we've done so far and highlight Danielle's talk about the Mona Lisa."

"Oh," said Danielle, "really, it's not worth blogging about."

"It is," said Izzy. "That was the most interesting ten minutes about art I've ever heard."

"Dear me," droned a voice from just ahead of us, a voice that was slimier than slugs in syrup. "You four girlies back there are driving me mad with all your girlie talk about girlie stuff." It was my archenemy, that low-down rat Harry Lovecraft.

Muddy aimed a remark at Harry Lovecraft that can't be repeated here, but it included the words "girlie," "total," and "smash." Then he said to Izzy, "How are you going to upload things to your blog around here?"

"We're not exactly miles from nowhere, Muddy," said Izzy. "There are terminals in the café next to the hotel."

"I thought you said we should never use public computers?" I said. "They're a bad security risk."

"I've got a program that generates random passwords," said Izzy. "As long as you've got the program you can open all your private files, and it won't leave anything personal on the computer you've used. I've got it stored on my memory card, along with the photos."

"Izzyyyy," I said, ever so nicely. "While you're on the Internet, could you print me out some news reports on what's happening in the Iceman DeSalle trial back home?"

"No, I could not," said Izzy. "You have to pay by the minute in that café, and it's not cheap."

"Good grief," whined Harry Lovecraft from up ahead of us. "Can't you give it a rest, Smart? You're always on about crime!"

"Well, with you around, Harry," I said, "crime is never far from any of our minds."

He turned and sneered at me. I resisted the urge to shudder. We trudged on, quickening our pace as a thunderously dark gray cloud crept into view above the buildings that stood along the banks of the River Seine. Big droplets of rain began to plop onto our shoulders. We all turned up our collars and kept our eyes to the ground as we hurried along.

There was a little courtyard we had to walk across just before we reached the entrance to the hotel. About a dozen souvenir stalls were always set out along one side of the yard, and they were never short of customers, as there were several other hotels nearby as well as the Eiffel Tower. By the time we reached the courtyard, the shower was over and we were all shaking the rain off our coat sleeves.

As we passed the stalls and as Mrs. Penzler called out, "No, we're not stopping now, you can come back and waste your money later on," I spotted a photo opportunity for Izzy. A knot of Japanese tourists were buying berets—it was a scene that absolutely cried out to be printed into someone's school project and labeled "Visitors to Paris." I nudged Izzy, pointed out the tourists, and she reached into her pocket.

"Oh no!" she cried. "The camera's gone!"

Sure enough, her coat pocket was empty. Her voice had been loud enough to reach Mrs. Penzler at the front of the group, and everyone skidded to a halt as

Mrs. Penzler's umbrella went up in the air again like an exclamation mark.

"Has it dropped out of your pocket, Isobel?" said Mrs. Penzler, bustling her way back past pupils and teachers, her outstretched umbrella parting a route for her as she went.

"It must have," cried Izzy. "Oh no, I could have dropped it streets away! I'll never find it!"

"Not necessarily," said Mrs. Penzler. "You may

only have dropped it moments ago. Everyone! Look around! Search for the camera!"

Everyone started milling about, bent over. We must have looked like a bunch of chickens pecking around on a farm!

All I could see were the small flat blocks that paved the courtyard. Here and there, little puddles left over from the rain collected in dips and cracks.

I took a step back, and the heel of my shoe knocked against something. I turned to find a small silver camera lying on the ground at my feet. I scooped it up, signaling to the others that it had been found.

Izzy hurried over, took the camera, and clutched it to her chest. "Thank goodness for that!" she said. "Thanks, Saxby."

"Is it damaged?" said Muddy. "If it is, I'll have a go at fixing it."

Izzy turned the camera over in her hands. "The case isn't scratched. I think it's okay." She switched it on, and the screen at the back blinked into life. "Yes, it's fine."

"Good. Now, be more careful in the future, Isobel!" said Mrs. Penzler. "That's school property!"

Izzy used a fingernail to unhook a catch at the bottom of the camera. She flipped open a tiny hatch to reveal the battery compartment.

"Oh no!" she cried all over again. "The memory card's come out! It must have fallen out when the camera dropped from my pocket!"

Up went Mrs. Penzler's umbrella. "Wait everyone! Look around! Search for the memory card!"

Everyone went through the chicken routine once more. Everyone except me, that is. I'd suddenly realized that the memory card hadn't dropped out of the camera at all. It had been stolen.

Have you noticed what I'd noticed?

Izzy had needed to deliberately open up that little hatch in the base of the camera, the one that covered the battery compartment. Even if the hatch had flipped open when the camera fell from her pocket, and even if the memory card had then been jolted out of its slot, that hatch couldn't possibly have closed itself again, could it? Conclusion: Someone had closed the hatch up again. Which meant it was highly likely that this same someone had taken the memory card.

This wasn't proof that it had been stolen. After all, it was still possible that the memory card had come out by accident. However, the fact that everyone was doing their chicken impression but not finding any trace of the memory card suggested that I was correct.

I hurried over to Mrs. Penzler and told her about my suspicions. Up went Mrs. Penzler's umbrella. "Wait everyone! Stop looking around! Saxby says the memory card has been stolen!"

"I think you're right, Saxby," said Muddy. "We've covered every square inch of this courtyard, and there's no memory card lying around."

At that precise moment, I was feeling pretty pleased

with myself. My detective skills had uncovered a crime that might otherwise have gone unnoticed!

But now, looking back on it as I write this down, I wish I'd kept my big mouth shut. I wish I'd never spotted the problem with the hatch. Why? You'll find out later on.

"Who's got the camera's memory card?" boomed Mrs. Penzler. "Speak up now and punishment will be minimal. This is your last chance."

No answer. We all looked blankly at each other.

Mrs. Penzler made a sort of half-grunt, half-sigh, which somehow managed to contain the words "Right, if you want to do this the hard way, then the hard way it is!"

"Everyone turn out their pockets!" she called. "Here you are, I'll empty mine too! Teachers, check everyone and everything, please."

There was a general hubbub of grumbling and pocket-digging. The Japanese tourists, now wearing their nice new berets, smiled at us as if this was exactly the kind of weird behavior they expected to see from a bunch of English people.

Muddy's pockets were—as always—bulging to

the bursting point with all sorts of his homemade gizmos and gadgets. So within seconds he was cradling a whole heap of items in his arms, including a small ball of string and a flashlight with what looked like a rifle sight on it.

The ball of string tumbled past his elbow, unraveling around his legs and bouncing away behind him as if it was making a dash for freedom. He tried to catch it, but with so much stuff balanced in each hand and the string looped around his ankles, he suddenly toppled over with a yell.

He crashed into the nearest of the souvenir stands, knocking it over and sending the vendor's assortment of ornaments, hats, and knickknacks scattering across the ground. It was pure luck that nothing was broken. Muddy apologized, quite a few times, and started putting everything back in place.

Danielle quickly went over and helped him. The vendor, a sour-looking fellow with a mustache and a leather overcoat that came down past his knees, glared at the pair of them. He muttered angrily to himself, then he muttered angrily to the stallholders next to him, then they muttered angrily in agreement.

After a couple of minutes, the souvenir stand was back to normal, everyone's pockets and bags had been checked, and Mrs. Penzler was pointing her umbrella again, this time at me.

"You've got it wrong, Saxby. The memory card isn't in anyone's possession and it isn't lying around. It must have been dropped after all. Isobel, I'm very disappointed. You were entrusted with the camera, and now we'll have no photographs when we get back to class, thanks to your carelessness."

Izzy went a shade of red usually reserved for tomatoes.

I didn't think Mrs. Penzler's search had been thorough enough; after all, that memory card could have been slipped into a shoe, or even hidden in a hairdo! I was about to point this out to her, but then thought better of it. It was hardly practical to start checking each other's socks in the middle of the street, was it? Besides, we could have a bank of X-ray machines and the thief might still have found a hiding place. No, best keep quiet for the moment, I thought.

"Come along now everyone!" declared Mrs. Penzler. "Or we'll be late for lunch, or in French, *le déjeuner*!

Danielle, come away from that stand, right now! We've bothered that poor man enough; you can buy souvenirs later."

The slippery tones of that low-down rat Harry Lovecraft drifted across the courtyard. "Well, well, Smart made a fool of himself. Bound to happen, sooner or later."

I felt like following the vendor's example and doing some angry muttering. I was sure that memory card had been deliberately taken. One or another of us had it.

I spent most of lunchtime scribbling notes and thinking.

Something doesn't add up. Why steal the memory card, but not the camera? If the thief had simply kept the camera, everyone would have assumed that Izzy had dropped it and that it was lost. No crime would have been discovered. Whoever took the card must have placed the camera on the ground where I found it.

SUPPECTS: Who did it? Could have been anyone! We were all milling about, looking at the ground. Anybody could have placed that camera there!

MOTIVE: Why take the card? Why steal a load of photos of Paris? Unless... could there have been something dodgy _in_ one of the photos? Did Izzy photograph something suspicious by mistake? Hmm, that seems unlikely.

WAIT! Izzy said her passcode program was on the card too. WAIT AGAIN! That low-down rat Harry Lovecraft was listening in! Is he up to his old tricks? Why would he want that passcode program? What sneaky plots could he hatch if he had access to it? _Must ask Izzy more about that._

CHAPTER THREE

After lunch, Mrs. Penzler let us all go souvenir hunting for half an hour. Most of the students—and most of the adults, come to think of it—headed straight back to the line of stands in the courtyard near the hotel.

Muddy, Izzy, and I headed for the stand Muddy had knocked over. He still felt very embarrassed and thought he ought to buy something from the vendor by way of another apology.

The man appeared to have cheered up a bit, and greeted us with a hearty couple of sentences which I think translated as, "Hello again, young friends. Have you come to encase watering cans in jam?"

As you can tell, my command of the French language isn't exactly great. What we'd done so far at school was fine if you wanted to point out a tree, or eat a carrot, but not so good for buying souvenirs from Parisian salesmen. We smiled politely at him and took a look at the items on his stall. In all, there were half a dozen scale models of the Louvre, a whole load of Mona Lisa posters, four Eiffel-Tower-shaped piggy banks, a vast array of Eiffel Tower key rings, various heavily packaged snow globes containing Parisian landmarks, and lots of scarves in different colors with the word "Paris!" sewn across them in huge letters.

In the end, all three of us bought Eiffel Tower piggy banks. They were about eight inches tall and brilliantly detailed. We handed over a disturbingly large number of Euros and went on our way.

"I'm sure he doubled the price, because it was us," said Izzy quietly.

"Still, they're brilliantly detailed," said Muddy. He was so busy admiring his piggy bank that a couple of steps later he collided with that low-down rat Harry Lovecraft.

"Dear me," said Harry, theatrically dusting himself off. "You seem to be making a habit of bumping into things today, Whitehouse. What's that you've got there?"

Muddy proudly displayed his piggy bank, and Harry took a close look at it. "Oh, I see," said Harry, "you put the coins in at the top. Yes, that's rather nice, actually. Beautifully detailed."

Muddy held the piggy bank close to his chest, as if worried that Harry might snatch it at any moment. Izzy pointed to the paper bag Harry was carrying.

"And what have you been buying?" she said.

Out of the paper bag, Harry produced a large plastic lunchbox, with pictures of Notre Dame Cathedral printed on it. Just the sort of junk you'd expect a cheapskate like Harry Lovecraft to buy.

"Nice," I said.

Harry walked—or should I say slithered?—away,

but not before he'd taken another good look at the piggy bank.

"Seeing that low-down rat reminds me," I said to Izzy. "I need to ask you about the password program you had on that missing memory card."

"Do we have to talk about that?" she said. "I feel terrible about losing it. We've lost every single picture I took!"

"If someone stole that password program," I said, "would they be able to use it to get into other people's Internet files?"

Izzy frowned. "Hmm. Not easily. The program itself is password protected, but if you knew exactly what sites to log on to and whose information you were after, then, yes. In theory."

"Thanks," I said. "That's veeeeeery interesting."

So here was a possible motive for stealing the memory card! I was so wrapped up in my own thoughts that now it was my turn to collide with someone. In this case, Danielle.

Or rather, she collided with me. She was hurrying across the courtyard toward the souvenir stands.

"Sorry!" she smiled. "I was miles away, I was

just . . . " She suddenly stared at Muddy's piggy bank. "Did you get that at one of these stands?"

"Yes," said Izzy brightly, "all three of us bought one."

Danielle's smile had vanished. "They're . . . really nice . . . aren't they . . ."

"Beautifully detailed," agreed Muddy.

Suddenly, the sound of Mrs. Penzler's rapidly clapping hands pulled us to attention. She was advancing across the courtyard, umbrella tucked under her arm.

"Come along, everyone! No more time for idle chatter! Form a line, we're now heading back toward the Champs Elysées. At the northern end of this stands the Arc de Triomphe, and at the other end is . . ."

Blah blah blah, and we were on the road again. It was an uneventful afternoon full of geography and history, followed by an uneventful evening full of worksheets and pizza.

It was the following morning when everything went ka-blam.

CHAPTER FOUR

The rooms at the Hotel Marseilles were assigned so that there were four boys or four girls to each one. I was in with Muddy and two boys from the other class in our year group.

It was two minutes to breakfast time. Muddy and I had our suitcases opened up on our hastily made beds, while we sorted through the jumble of clothes inside. Muddy had come up with the excellent idea of keeping those piggy banks of ours wrapped up inside a couple of socks, so they wouldn't get damaged on the return journey. We sat our sock bundles on top of our clothes.

"Honestly, Muddy," I tutted, "you should keep your clean clothes separate. How are you going to know which ones you've already worn?"

"Well, the worn ones are all crumpled up," said Muddy.

"Yes, but you've got your clean ones all crumpled up too."

"Oh yeah. I'll just have to sniff them or something."

"You really are a walking pigsty," I muttered.

"Quick!" cried Muddy, looking at his watch. "Breakfast!"

Leaving everything as it was, we dashed out of the room and took the stairs four at a time, joining the stampede for breakfast. There was no way I was going to be late for those really tasty little bread rolls with the chocolate bits inside! The other guests at the hotel flinched as the entire St. Egbert's gang flooded into the dining room.

"What do they call those things?" I said, three minutes later, as I bit into my third really tasty little bread roll with the chocolate bits inside.

"Aren't they pain au chocolat?" mumbled Muddy through a mouthful of freshly baked croissant.

"No," I said, "I think those are the pastry things with chocolate bits inside."

Izzy appeared, a worried expression on her face.

"Hi," I said. "Is Danielle not with you?"

"No," said Izzy, "I've not seen her. Saxby, my suitcase has been searched."

I stopped in mid-chew. "Are you sure?"

"Positive. I came back from the bathroom and my case had definitely been gone through."

"What about the others in your room?" said Muddy.

"The room was empty for about ten minutes before I returned," said Izzy. "I've asked the others, but nobody saw anything and none of their stuff has been touched."

"Was anything taken?" I said.

"No," said Izzy. "Nothing. I don't understand it."

I was about to ask Izzy if she was sure she hadn't simply made a mistake, when Mrs. Penzler scooted into view.

"Attention, St. Egbert's! Has anyone seen my wristwatch? I thought I'd left it on my bedside cabinet last night, but as it wasn't there this morning I think I must have lost it while I was timing you doing your worksheets last night. Anyone? Anyone?"

Everyone shrugged and shook their head.

"Honestly," she grumbled, "first we lose all our photos and now I lose my watch."

The look of annoyance-but-not-distress on Mrs. Penzler's face told me that she was assuming it was lost rather than stolen. Mind you, she still thought the memory card was lost rather than stolen. And now there was also the question of what was going on with Izzy's suitcase. I looked around the room. A certain low-down rat was noticeable by his absence.

After breakfast, we all went back to our rooms to collect anything we'd need to take with us on today's outing (by train, to the Palais de Versailles, a few miles outside the city). As Muddy and I sat on our beds, everything appeared normal: beds hastily made, bags on beds, clothes in bags, piggy banks poking out from under clothes, coats on hooks by the door, Muddy's gadgets in a heap beside his bed . . .

But I knew that something had happened in here while we'd been having breakfast. Have you spotted it too?

"Somebody's searched through our stuff as well," I said.

"How do you know that?" said Muddy, picking a pair of underpants out of the pile in his bag.

"We left those piggy banks sitting on top of our clothes," I said. "And we left them wrapped up in socks, too. Now they're poking out from underneath the clothes. Someone's been looking through our luggage, just like they've looked through Izzy's."

"Why unwrap our piggy banks?" said Muddy. "They're only souvenirs."

I lifted my Eiffel Tower-shaped piggy bank from my suitcase and turned it over in my hands. Nothing odd about it. Nothing unusual. Slot at the top, plastic plug at the base, nothing inside, no distinguishing markings on it.

I frowned. Some odd things were happening, and so far I had no idea what might link them all together. However, there was one thought that kept going around and around in my head.

"Stealing things if the chance presents itself," I muttered. "Searching through people's bags. Doesn't that remind you of someone?"

"It's exactly the sort of thing Harry Lovecraft's got up to in the past," said Muddy.

"And he wasn't at breakfast." I stood up. "Let's go and have a word with him."

We only had a few minutes before we had to be in the hotel lobby, ready to leave for the day. Right on cue, as we approached Harry's room at the other end of the corridor, Harry came sauntering toward us.

"Where were you during breakfast?" I said.

"None of your business, Smart," sneered Harry.

"Things are going missing," I said. "Bags are being searched."

"And you assume it's my doing?" said Harry. "How nice. How very fair-minded of you."

"Why did you miss breakfast?" said Muddy. "What were you up to?"

"I didn't miss breakfast," said Harry. "I went down early."

"Why?" I said.

Harry looked at me as if I was giving off a terrible smell. "Not that it's anything to do with you, Smart, but I wanted to leave time to mail two souvenirs I've bought. If you give parcels in at the reception desk, they'll take them to the post office for you."

"Why mail souvenirs back home?" I said.

"Because it's more interesting than sending a postcard, that's why!" sneered Harry. "If you must know, it's my stepmother's birthday tomorrow and I'd forgotten to get her anything."

"How many stepmothers have you had now?" I said. "Two?"

"Three," said Harry, with a smile like a python. "This one I really like, actually."

"Don't believe you," said Muddy.

Harry tutted and pulled a folded sheet of paper from his pocket. He handed it to me. It was a receipt, for one parcel, addressed to a Mrs. P. Lovecraft, written on Hotel Marseilles notepaper, stamped, and signed by the hotel receptionist.

"Oh," I said feebly.

"Oh dear," smarmed Harry. "Looks like you've got it wrong again, Smart. All this playing at detectives you do, and you still can't tell the guilty from the innocent. Oh dear."

He skipped away down the stairs.

If I'd been one of those American tough-guy detectives from the 1940s, I'd probably have given him a thump in the face. But I wasn't. So I didn't.

Instead, I immediately came to an uncomfortable conclusion. There was only one other person who hadn't been at breakfast, which meant that there was only one other person who could have had the opportunity to search those three suitcases . . .

At breakfast, I'd asked Izzy where Danielle was, and Izzy said she hadn't seen her. But why would Danielle be searching our bags? Had she stolen the memory card? Had she stolen Mrs. Penzler's watch? And why? My brain suddenly contained more questions than one of Mrs. Penzler's math tests!

I hoped I was wrong. Well, okay, wrong again. I hoped I'd discover that Danielle had an alibi, as Harry did, and that she could prove she was doing something during breakfast that hadn't involved rifling through other people's luggage.

When everyone assembed in the hotel's reception area a few minutes later, Danielle finally appeared. Izzy went over to her, and I crept closer to them to acciden-tally-on-purpose overhear what they were saying.

"Hi," said Izzy. "You okay? You weren't at break-fast."

"Fine," said Danielle hurriedly. "I, er, wasn't hun-gry . . ."

What? When there were those really tasty little bread rolls with the chocolate bits inside on the menu?

I didn't believe her for even a fraction of a split nanosecond. So much for having an alibi! But what could Danielle possibly be up to? Stealing was totally out of character for her. Or, so it seemed.

Danielle appeared even more quiet than usual. I got the distinct impression that something was bothering her. I also got the distinct impression she'd been crying.

There's a strange mismatch here: Danielle appears to be acting just like Harry Lovecraft (apart from the tears) and Harry Lovecraft appears to be acting like someone who's got nothing to hide.

Assuming for a moment that <u>Danielle</u> took the watch, etc. The big question is <u>why?</u> What could be her <u>motive?</u>

Assuming for a moment that <u>Harry</u> took the watch, etc. (there's no real need to ask why—this is that lowdown rat Harry Lovecraft we're talking about) Why get up to his old tricks here? If he's out to steal stuff, where's he hiding it?

BAM! KAPOW! I've got it! That lunchbox he bought—the one with pictures of Notre Dame cathedral on it! He's just posted a parcel back home and that lunchbox would be ideal for hiding things in! What a brilliant way to dispose of stolen loot—post it home!

No, wait. What about his alibi covering the time when those bags were searched? What about the fact that Danielle has no alibi? Why was nothing taken from those bags? I am very confused. Must get to sleep now. I'm writing these notes by flashlight.

CHAPTER FIVE

My eyes flashed open. It was still very early in the morning, and everything in the room around me was a series of pale outlines and dark shadows. A few feet away, Muddy suddenly grunt-snored and turned over in his sleep.

The problem of the stolen items and searched bags had haunted my mind all night, but a thought had now occurred to me that at least gave me a firm theory to work on.

Readers of my earlier case file *The Mark of the Purple Homework* will remember that Harry Lovecraft had bullied a classmate into doing his dirty work for him. It struck me that the same thing might be happening here. That low-down rat had some sort of hold over Danielle! He'd made her steal the memory card and the watch, and he'd made her search through that luggage for valuables. Meanwhile, he could stand back and give himself an alibi whenever he needed it.

Yes, that theory fitted the facts! It certainly accounted for why Danielle had been looking so upset. It didn't answer the question of why nothing had been taken from the bags, but perhaps it was simply a case of nothing being found that was worth lifting?

At breakfast, I quietly alerted Izzy and Muddy. I told them to keep a close watch on both Danielle and Harry.

"I need more evidence," I whispered. "At the moment, it's only a theory."

"Sounds like a pretty convincing one," whispered Muddy.

"Poor Danielle," whispered Izzy. "What could that low-down rat be threatening her with?"

"That's what we've got to find out," I whispered, as Danielle appeared and headed for our table. Izzy waved and beckoned her over. She was still looking distinctly unhappy, and the dark patches under her eyes told me she'd had even less sleep than me.

After another fruitless nose around the hotel looking for her wristwatch, Mrs. Penzler announced that we'd have a free morning—the teachers would be available to take small groups out and about, wherever they wanted to go. And no, she said firmly, that did not include Disneyland.

Once all the "awww"s had died down, everyone organized themselves into batches. Muddy volunteered to stick with whatever group Harry Lovecraft was in: a group going back up the Eiffel Tower, as it turned out, which pleased Muddy enormously. I stuck with Danielle: a whole bunch of girls going shopping, as it turned out. Which did not please me enormously.

Never mind, there were more important issues at stake here. When the opportunity arose, I planned to take Danielle to one side, tell her about my suspicions, and assure her that whatever trouble she was having with Harry, I was here to help.

An opportunity arose sooner than I expected. And this opportunity involved the first of three eye-popping shocks that blew the whole case wide open!

Eye-popping shock number one:

Only moments after leaving the hotel, my group crossed that courtyard containing all those souvenir stands. The girls immediately scattered, to descend on the stands like a swarm of T-shirt-buying locusts.

Danielle headed for the guy in the leather overcoat, the one whose stall had got knocked over by Muddy. She seemed flustered and was trying to ask him about something. However, he couldn't speak a word of English, and she couldn't speak a word of French (I don't think they'd done any French at her previous school, and as she'd only been at St. Egbert's a few weeks, she'd hardly had time to learn how to say hello).

Their "conversation" was getting increasingly heated and confused. I hurried over to Danielle.

"Hi, can I help?"

Danielle almost jumped out of her skin. "Oh! Er, no, thanks, it's fine, Saxby, thanks."

"I can translate your question, if you like," I said. "Of course, I might ask the guy if I can borrow his pig's wellies, or something, but I can give it a go."

"No, really," said Danielle hurriedly, "thanks, but no, I was only seeing if he had any more of the postcard packs he had the other day."

I knew at once that she was lying and that she was covering up whatever it was she really wanted to ask him.

Have you spotted it too?

There were no postcards on that stand the other day. I'd taken a good look when Izzy, Muddy, and I had bought those Eiffel Tower piggy banks. Speaking of those piggy banks, I now noticed that the vendor had sold the fourth and last of them.

The piggy banks! I suddenly remembered that Harry had particularly admired those piggy banks! He knew that Izzy, Muddy, and I had each bought one. He must have made Danielle go searching through our bags, to steal one for him. But Danielle, being honest, hadn't had the heart to do it. Harry had obviously threatened her again, and so here she was, back at the souvenir stand, trying to BUY one for him instead.

I took her to one side. And here's the eye-popping shock, coming up right now.

"Danielle," I said quietly. "I know Harry's been bullying you over something. He's done it before. But don't worry, I can help you stop him."

"Stop who?" she said.

"Harry. Harry Lovecraft."

She looked blankly at me. She genuinely didn't know what I was talking about. Eye-popping shock! "Is he the boy with the shiny hair and the shiny shoes?"

"Y-yes," I stammered. "You mean, he hasn't threatened you?"

"What?" she blinked. "No, absolutely not. What are you going on about?" She walked away quickly, joining some of the other girls at a nearby stand.

What? What? But if . . . That meant . . . I didn't . . . W-what?

Eye-popping shock number two:

A couple of minutes later, as the girls were grabbing up the last of the stock from the souvenir stands, Mrs. Penzler led her group through the courtyard. They were heading, at a brisk pace, to the area around Sacré-Coeur to see the street artists at work.

"Mrs. Penzler," I cried, "you've got your watch on!"

"Yes, Saxby!" she said, not slowing down for a second. "I went back to my room and looked again, and there it was, wedged down between the mattress and the headboard of my bed. I knew it had to be around somewhere. Come along, my group, we'll take the Metro north!"

Eye-popping shock! If that watch was never stolen in the first place . . . But that would mean that . . . How did that . . .?

Eye-popping shock number three:

Still reeling from the first two eye-popping shocks, I got permission to retreat to the café next to the hotel. I thought I'd catch up on the DeSalle trial back home, to take my mind off the wild criss-cross of thoughts that were now bouncing around inside my head.

I paid for ten minutes of Internet access, looked up one of the English news sites, and printed out the latest report. I read it on my way back to the hotel.

DESALLE TRIAL HEATS UP

On day four of the trial of Frank "Iceman" DeSalle and nine other defendants, the court was given details of how DeSalle, along with his personal lawyer Jeffrey Ffoules-Hampstead and his personal trainer Bob Trackenfield, are alleged to have conned thirty-six old ladies out of their life savings and stolen cash from shops when the assistants weren't looking.

It was claimed by an undercover police officer, Sgt. Donna Fitzgerald, that

Mr. DeSalle personally took money from 97-year-old Mrs. Edith Nesbit and used this money to buy racing cars, expensive holidays, and items from the SwordStore catalogue. An expert witness, the senior accountant Mr. Colin Plummley, was called to give evidence. He demonstrated the methods that DeSalle and his personal chef, Joey "Bug-Face" Smith, are alleged to have used to conceal these illegal activities, swapping cash through various bank accounts in order to hide it.

Two further witnesses—Veronica Clarke and Harold King, both ex-members of the DeSalle gang—gave evidence to support yesterday's allegations that Mr. DeSalle and his personal hairdresser, William Nickleby, robbed four security trucks, three lorries carrying items of jewelry, and an ice cream van (although this last crime is said to have been a case of mistaken identity). These witnesses also made statements regarding the claims

that Mr. DeSalle used his FaceSpace web
page to contact fellow criminals using
coded messages.

Mr. DeSalle and the other defendants
deny all charges. The case continues.

I was glad I'd taken time out like this. What an enter-
tainingly stupid bunch of crooks the DeSalle gang
were! Naturally, if I'd been on the case, I'd have . . .

Hang on. I read through the report again. Eye–
popping shock! There was a direct personal connection between the DeSalle trial and the people here, on
the St. Egbert's school trip to Paris!

Have you noticed it?

Danielle again! Her surname was Plummley. The only personal information she'd let slip was that her dad was an accountant (see Chapter Two!). And an accountant called Colin Plummley had been called as an expert witness in the trial (an expert witness is someone who has no actual connection with the trial, but who knows a lot about a particular subject—in this case, money matters—and so can advise the court).

Okay, Plummley wasn't that unusual a name, and there was probably more than one Mr. Plummley in the world who worked as an accountant. But it was enough of a coincidence to start ringing the bell marked: Uh-oh, there's something else going on here.

Suddenly, like snow settling on the roof of my shed on a winter's day, the pieces of the entire puzzle fell delicately into place. Standing there, on that street corner in Paris, I realized exactly what had been going on. I also realized that I would need to have a quiet word with Harry Lovecraft and with Danielle, and then say nothing to anyone until we were all back at school the following week.

How much of it can you piece together?

CHAPTER SIX

Exactly one week later, at 8:50 a.m., back at St. Egbert's, the bell rang for the start of school, and there was a mighty scraping of chair legs and shuffling of feet as my class settled itself down. Mrs. Penzler tapped her ruler for silence.

"Before registration, Saxby has asked me if he can talk to you. As you all know, since the memory card of the school's camera was lost in Paris, we've been unable to use any pictures in our follow-up projects . . . "

Izzy went tomato-red with embarrassment again.

". . . But Saxby claims to have located the card. How, I can't imagine. You'd better be right about this, Saxby."

Murmurs rippled through the classroom. Half of

them were murmuring with excitement, and half of them were murmuring with disbelief.

"Oh, I'm sure I'm right," I said, hopping up to the front of the class with my school bag. "Well, pretty sure. Before I continue, I'd better say that I've asked Danielle Plummley's permission to tell you this . . ." Everyone looked at Danielle. ". . . and I've, er, done a deal with Harry Lovecraft that will help me prove what I'm telling you is true."

Everyone looked at Harry. He was aiming a slimy grin at me. He clearly thought I was about to make a fool of myself again and was loving every minute of it.

"As you've probably all seen on the news," I said, "the trial of Frank 'Iceman' DeSalle ended yesterday. The whole gang was sent to prison for years. Open and shut case. Nasty bunch of crooks, got what they deserved. Naturally, I'd have solved the case in half the time, but, er, that's beside the point. 'What has that news story got to do with us?' I hear you say. Well, quite a lot. The DeSalle trial is what led to the vanishing of that memory card."

Another ripple of murmurs spread across the classroom. This time it was nearly all murmurs of disbelief.

"And here's how," I said. "Danielle Plummley has only been at St. Egbert's for a few weeks. Up to now, we've known her as a shy, quiet member of our class. And that's because she's had a secret. Her dad, a well-respected accountant, was called to be an expert witness in the DeSalle trial. His evidence was vital when it came to finding DeSalle and his henchmen guilty.

"Now, as you can imagine, any honest, law-abiding man who spends his days talking about bank statements, pension funds, and savings and loan association interest rates isn't exactly Mr. Wild and Exciting. No offense, Danielle . . . "

"None taken."

". . . Mr. Plummley leads a sensible, quiet life. By nature, he's a reserved sort of person, rather like his daughter. So suddenly finding himself dragged into the world of high-powered crime was a bit of a shock. He knew he shouldn't refuse to be an expert witness: after all, if DeSalle and his gang were going to be successfully jailed, the police would need Mr. Plummley's advice. He saw it as his duty to help, just as any of us would.

"However, the Plummleys are also no different from the rest of us in that they'd heard stories. Stories about crooks threatening witnesses, stories about criminal gangs taking revenge on anyone who crossed them. Stories like that are headline news.

"In the DeSalle case, something like that was very unlikely to happen to the Plummleys. For one thing, Mr. Plummley was only giving the court his expert opinion, he wasn't an actual witness to the crimes. And for another thing, the DeSalle mob might have been nasty little lowlifes, but they'd never resorted to beatings, or murders, or anything like that.

"But the Plummleys don't know that. They see the headline news like the rest of us. So, of course, they're nervous. Until DeSalle is locked up in prison, they're worried about their safety.

"What's more, they've recently moved to a new house, and Danielle is about to go to a new school, this school. Mr. and Mrs. Plummley, not knowing how far the tentacles of the DeSalle gang reach, tell Danielle that under no circumstances is she to tell anyone at her new school about the trial. Just stay silent, they say, until the trial is over. We're in a new town and we don't know anyone and we should play it safe.

"So, Danielle arrives in school and much as we like her, we find she's not saying anything about herself or her family. In fact, the one and only piece of information that she lets slip is the fact that her dad's an accountant.

"And then, the school trip to Paris is announced. Danielle's parents tell her she can't go, it's too much of a risk. What if DeSalle's henchmen decide to strike? No, they don't want Danielle off in a foreign country at exactly the time when the trial will be taking place. But Danielle is desperate to go. She's studied art history, it's a subject she loves. She really, really, really wants to go to Paris and see the Louvre and all the fabulous art that's in it.

"Reluctantly, her parents agree to let her go. On the understanding that, while she's away, her silence on the DeSalle case is more important than ever. Danielle promises them she'll stick to the plan.

"So, a few days later, we're in Paris. On our visit to the Louvre, Danielle suddenly dazzles us with her knowledge of the Mona Lisa and Leonardo da Vinci. She can't help herself, it's her favorite topic in the entire world. The rest of us are hugely impressed.

"And here's where it starts to go wrong. Walking back to the hotel, Izzy announces she's going to blog the whole Paris trip and make a special feature of Danielle's talk at the Louvre. What's more, the blog is going to appear on FaceSpace, the same Web site that figures in the DeSalle trial. In other words, Danielle Plummley, daughter of expert witness Colin Plummley, is about to get featured on a Web site that the DeSalle gang themselves use, and which is getting a lot of attention because of the DeSalle trial.

"Danielle panics. She simply can't tell us all the truth, but at the same time she can't allow that blog to get uploaded revealing the school she now attends and the area her family lives in. So she does the only thing she can think of: she sneaks the school camera out of Izzy's pocket and takes the memory card. Why? Because she's heard, during our conversation, that Izzy's password program is needed to access her blog and that the password program is on the memory card of the school camera.

"Danielle intends to keep the card for only a few days, until the trial is over. She hates the idea of stealing it, but what else can she do? Unfortunately, before she can get the camera back into Izzy's pocket, it's noticed that the camera is gone.

"We all search for it. When nobody's looking, Danielle puts the camera on the ground, where I find it. Now, if I'd kept my big mouth shut, that might have been the end of it. The memory card would be lost and then, after the trial, found again. But no, I had to do my detective bit. I spotted that the memory card had been deliberately taken.

"So, everyone is made to turn out their pockets. Poor Danielle panics again. The memory card will now be found, and found in her pocket. Either she gets labeled a thief, or she has to tell the truth. What can she do? Okay, with hindsight, maybe telling Mrs. Penzler quietly what was going on might have saved a lot of trouble. But Danielle's the new girl. She doesn't really know any of us, including the teachers. And she's under strict instructions not to let the cat out of the bag!

"On the point of Danielle's secret being discovered, she has a bit of luck. Muddy knocks over a souvenir stand on which there are, among other things, four Eiffel Tower piggy banks. Spotting her chance, Danielle rushes over to help Muddy pick everything up and, while doing so, she slips the memory card into the coin slot of one of the piggy banks. She decides to simply buy the piggy bank and retrieve the card. In the meantime, the card isn't found in the search and Danielle's secret remains safe.

"As soon as the search is done, she goes over to the stand to buy the piggy bank. But Mrs. Penzler calls her away. She is forced to leave it where it is for now.

"A little while later, after lunch, we all go souvenir hunting. By the time Danielle can return to the stand, all four of the piggy banks have been sold! She's very upset—she thinks the memory card is gone forever. But then she discovers that Izzy, Muddy, and I have ALL bought those same Eiffel Tower piggy banks."

"So where did the fourth one go?" said Mrs. Penzler.

"Ah, I'll get to that in a minute," I said. "Danielle now reasons to herself that there's a very good chance the memory card is inside one of those three. During breakfast the next morning, she sneaks into Izzy's room, and then into my and Muddy's room, to open up the piggy banks and check. But, all three turn out to be empty. Danielle realizes that the memory card was in the fourth piggy bank. It's now well and truly gone—there's no way she'll be able to catch up with that fourth Eiffel Tower now.

"When the searched-through suitcases are discovered, I start putting two and two together and making five and a half. I start suspecting that Harry Lovecraft is up to his old tricks, especially when Mrs. Penzler's watch goes missing too. I suspect that Harry is threatening Danielle in some way, and getting her to steal things for him."

I cleared my throat. This next bit wasn't going to be easy.

"Okay," I said, "as part of my deal with Harry, I'm now going to . . . apologize to Harry . . . in public . . . for suspecting him."

More murmurs across the classroom. Harry eyed me gleefully. He really was enjoying this enormously.

"Harry was entirely innocent," I said. "I realized it when three eye-popping shocks turned up one after the other. The decider was the report on the DeSalle trial I downloaded in the café next door to the hotel. It showed me the connection between Danielle and the trial, and the entire truth suddenly dawned on me."

"But where is the memory card?" said Mrs. Penzler. "You claimed you'd tracked it down."

"And so I have," I said. I reached down and pulled a parcel out of my bag. This was the same package Harry Lovecraft had mailed back home from the Hotel Marseilles.

"As the other part of my deal with Harry," I said, "he's let me have this package he sent from Paris. It wasn't opened when it arrived, as his stepmother had just walked out on his dad for forgetting her birthday again. At my request, Harry has left it sealed up.

"You see, I saw Danielle talking to the owner of that souvenir stand on the day after the suitcases were searched. If she'd found the memory card in one of the first three

Eiffel Towers, she wouldn't have needed to return to the stand at all, but she was making one last attempt to find out where that fourth Eiffel Tower had gone.

"Seeing her there, I thought she was trying to buy the last of the Eiffel Tower piggy banks for Harry. Why did I think that? Because only moments after Izzy, Muddy, and I bought our piggy banks, we bumped into Harry. He made it clear that he liked those piggy banks very much.

"What I hadn't realized was that Harry, straight after we'd bumped into him, went over to that stand and bought the last piggy bank, the fourth one, for himself. That was why Danielle had found all four of them gone, two days before! That was why she was upset after she couldn't find the memory card in the first three piggy banks. That was why she thought the memory card was now gone forever.

"Harry told me he'd mailed two souvenirs back home. I should have listened to him more carefully. I should have asked him what that second souvenir was. But I didn't. Quite innocently, Harry had bought the fourth piggy bank, the one with the memory card hidden inside it.

"And now, if I'm right, we can retrieve all our lost photos and this whole mystery will be concluded."

I borrowed a pair of scissors from Mrs. Penzler and snipped open Harry's parcel. From inside the brown paper wrapping I pulled his lunchbox with pictures of Notre Dame on it. I opened the lunchbox . . .

. . . And inside, wrapped in birthday paper (and with a note from Harry to his ex-stepmom saying: The lunch-box is mine, it's just protecting this present.) was the fourth of those Eiffel Tower piggy banks. Flipping the piggy bank over, I removed the plastic cap from its base, held my hand out, and gave the piggy bank a shake.

A small blue memory card dropped into my hand. The class erupted in a mixture of yells and applause. I gave Harry his lunchbox and piggy bank, and I gave Izzy her memory card. She looked like she was about to kiss me, so I took a step back, just in case.

"Saxby, you're a genius," she said.

"I know," I said.

After such a brilliant series of deductions, I'd expected to be the center of attention for the rest of the day. But no, everyone flocked around Danielle. They wanted to hear every last detail of the DeSalle case. By break time, Danielle Plummley was the most popular girl in the school. The only fly in the ointment was that Harry Lovecraft was even more smug and smarmy than usual. And probably would be for days. Oh well, at least this case had taught me not to jump to conclusions too quickly!

Later that day, I returned to my shed and my Thinking Chair. I'd missed it while I'd been away.

Case closed.

Simon Cheshire

spent over a decade working in the marketing departments of various publishing companies before quitting to become a full-time writer. Visit him at www.simoncheshire.co.uk.

R.W. Alley

is perhaps best known for illustrating the Paddington Bear books. He has also produced more than one hundred books, including most recently *There's a Princess in the Palace*, written by his wife Zoë. They live together in Barrington, Rhode Island.

Enjoy the other books in the
Saxby Smart series!

THE CURSE OF THE ANCIENT MASK
AND OTHER CASE FILES
By Simon Cheshire · Pictures by R.W. Alley

978-1-59643-474-5

$15.99

"After reading this well-paced and sometimes funny first-person narrative, young mystery fans will be looking for the second volume in the Saxby Smart Private Detective series." *–Booklist*

THE TREASURE OF DEAD MAN'S LANE
AND OTHER CASE FILES
By Simon Cheshire · Pictures by R.W. Alley

978-1-59643-475-2

$15.99

★"Outstanding fare for young armchair Sherlocks."
–Booklist, starred review

FRIENDS FREE LIBRARY
GERMANTOWN FRIENDS LIBRARY
5418 Germantown Avenue
Philadelphia, PA 19144
215-951-2355

Each borrower is responsible for all items
checked out on his/her library card, for
fines on materials kept overtime, and
replacing any lost or damaged materials.